THE CLAWS THAT REND . . .

Jupiter Monk began cracking the whip to the left side of the Red Devil, hoping to move it to the right. It took two steps, then stood motionless while the whip touched it again.

Then, without a sound, it hurled itself straight at the animal trainer. Monk held the chair out, only to see it go flying across the cage. He flicked the whip, but the Red Devil paid it no attention. It stalked him, belly to ground, soundlessly, oblivious to the noise and pain of the whip, and Monk began backing away toward the cage door.

Suddenly the Red Devil leaped right past him and positioned itself by the door. And now the stalk continued, as the creature, silent as death, its red eyes gleaming, backed Monk up against the bars, and slowly, cruelly, prepared for the kill. . . .

SIGNET Science Fiction You'll Enjoy

THE THREE-LEGGED HOOTCH DANCER

Tales of the Galactic Midway #2

by
Mike Resnick

A SIGNET BOOK
NEW AMERICAN LIBRARY
TIMES MIRROR

NAL BOOKS ARE AVAILABLE AT QUANTITY DISCOUNTS WHEN USED
TO PROMOTE PRODUCTS OR SERVICES. FOR INFORMATION PLEASE
WRITE TO PREMIUM MARKETING DIVISION, THE NEW AMERICAN
LIBRARY, INC., 1633 BROADWAY, NEW YORK, NEW YORK 10019.

SIGNET TRADEMARK REG. U.S. PAT. OFF. AND FOREIGN COUNTRIES
REGISTERED TRADEMARK—MARCA REGISTRADA
HECHO EN CHICAGO, U.S.A.

SIGNET, SIGNET CLASSICS, MENTOR, PLUME, MERIDIAN AND NAL BOOKS
are published by The New American Library, Inc.,
1633 Broadway, New York, New York 10019

First Printing, February, 1983

1 2 3 4 5 6 7 8 9

PRINTED IN THE UNITED STATES OF AMERICA

To Carol, as always,

and to John and Louise Cain,
with friendship and affection

1.

He was, by choice, a Thing.

Where once he had arms and legs and long lean fingers, now he had two soft gray lumps. There was nothing—neither stubs nor even scars—to indicate that his legs had ever existed. The smooth bronzed skin that had once covered his body was gone, replaced by coarse gray reticulations that exuded a foul-smelling slime. His nose, once short and narrow, was now a broad, wrinkled band of cartilage, the nostrils fully eight inches apart. If he possessed eyes, no observer could tell. His mouth, which had once dined on steak, was now equipped only for sucking fluids. Clouds of vapor engulfed him whenever he exhaled.

His name was John Edward Carp, and he was content.

2.

"Somehow," sighed Thaddeus Flint, popping open a can of beer and surveying the bleak, barren, red-brown landscape, "this wasn't exactly what I had in mind when I set this deal up."

"Surely you didn't think that every world would be like your own, Mr. Flint," said his tall, cadaverous, blue-skinned partner with what passed for a smile.

"As a matter of fact, I had rather hoped one or two of them might be *better*—or at least more interesting." Flint pulled a handkerchief out of his pocket and wiped the sweat from his face. "This is some galactic civilization you've got yourself, Mr. Ahasuerus. I don't think I've been this impressed since I passed through Biloxi in the winter."

The blue man shrugged. "View it as a shakedown tour. The Corporation wants to see what you can do in the sticks before they let you play the Big Lemon." Flint snorted, and Mr. Ahasuerus turned to him. "Didn't I say it right?"

"Close enough," replied Flint, taking a sip of his beer. "Well, where do we set up?"

"You're the expert," said Mr. Ahasuerus.

Flint looked around, then spat on the sandy loam. "This is as good a place as any. No water, no toilets, no roads, no people. Why should we make things easy for ourselves?"

"Do I detect a note of sarcasm?" asked the blue man mildly.

2

"Would you like me to sing it in E above high C, just so you'll be sure?" replied Flint. He saw a burly man leaning against the spaceship and called to him. "Hey, Swede!"

"Yeah, boss?"

"I realize that standing around sunning yourself is pretty important work, but if you can tear yourself away from it for a couple of hours, I want you to go into town, wherever *that* may be, and start posting signs to the effect that *The Ahasuerus and Flint Traveling Carnival and Sideshow* will be open for business at sunset."

"Anything else?" asked Swede.

"Just try not to get trampled in the mad rush," said Flint dryly. He turned back to the blue man. "I assume someone has made sure that the signs are in some language that the residents of this vacation spa can read—always assuming they have eyes, of course."

"It has been seen to," responded Mr. Ahasuerus.

"And Swede's not gonna get shot or strung up?"

"Not as an invading alien," said the blue man. "Of course, if they've had a prior unsatisfactory experience with a carnival . . ."

"Well," shrugged Flint, "that's why we're not sending someone real important, like you or me." He finished his beer, squeezed the can out of shape, and tossed it on the ground. "God, I don't know what I'm going to do when I run through the last of this stuff. You'd think *someone* in this goddamned galaxy would know how to brew a keg of beer!"

His gaze fell on Jupiter Monk, the big, ruddy-faced animal trainer. He was standing about two hundred yards from the ship, a huge hoop in his hand, waiting for Simba, his aging, near-toothless lion, to jump through it. Simba seemed more interested in watching the strippers unloading their costumes.

"Come on, you fucking overgrown alleycat!" bellowed Monk. "It ain't as if I've got all afternoon!"

Simba looked at him and yawned.

Monk shook the hoop in front of him and bellowed a nonstop stream of curses. Finally the lion sighed, crouched, and jumped unenthusiastically toward the hoop. His head hit the top of it, a forepaw hooked onto the rim, and Simba,

3

Monk, and the hoop went sprawling in a dusty, twitching heap.

"Goddammit, Thaddeus!" bellowed Monk, pulling lion hair out of his mouth and carefully rearranging his long, drooping mustache.

"What is it this time?" asked Flint wearily, walking over to the scene of the mini-disaster.

"Just once, I wish to hell you'd pick a world that has the same gravity as Earth! Now, that's not so fucking much to ask, is it?" Monk paused to remove a final hair from his mouth. "When you told me we were going to tour all these worlds, I thought it was going to be a little different, you know what I mean?"

Flint nodded. "I know exactly what you mean. Talk to my partner. He picks the worlds."

"He keeps picking worlds like this one and he's going to find himself with a little four-legged company in bed some night," said Monk. He sighed. "I could be watching the Cincinnati Bengals playing the Pittsburgh Steelers right now, you know that? I don't *need* this shit."

"Can you guess what *I* don't need right now?" asked Flint.

"I'm sorry," said Monk, brushing himself off. "But you got to admit this sure don't look like all those futuristic worlds we used to see in the movies."

"I know. How's the Dancer adjusting to the gravity?"

"How the hell do I know?" responded Monk. "I got problems of my own." He grimaced. "In point of fact, I got two leopards who stand a good chance of leaping clear out of the tent if I don't do a little work with 'em."

So saying, he reached down, grabbed Simba by his mane, and started leading him off in the direction of the animal cages.

Flint watched him for a moment, then sought out Billybuck Dancer, his trick-shot artist. The young man was sitting cross-legged on the ground, staring off at some fixed point in space and time that only he could see.

"How's it going, Dancer?" asked Flint, after standing in front of him for almost a minute without eliciting a response.

4

"Just fine," replied the Dancer in his gentle Texas drawl. "Everything's just fine, Thaddeus."

"Any problems with the gravity?"

"Naw."

"Have you practiced?" persisted Flint.

"Don't need to," responded the young man. "One world's pretty much like the next."

"You're going to be shooting a cigarette out of a girl's mouth at a hundred and fifty feet," continued Flint. "What if something goes wrong?"

"Nothing ever does."

"Damm it, Dancer!"

The young man sighed, got to his feet, and loosened the pistol he had tucked into his belt. Then he leaned down, picked up a trio of reddish stones, and hurled them high into the air.

"Am I supposed to be impressed?" asked Flint, as the stones reached their apex and started falling toward the ground.

The Dancer smiled and suddenly became a blur of motion. The three stones had been blown apart before Flint had even heard the first report of the gun.

"It's just like pointing your finger, Thaddeus," said the Dancer softly. He tucked the gun back into his belt, lowered himself to the ground, crossed his legs, and resumed staring off into the distance. Flint looked at him for a long moment, then smiled, shrugged, and walked over to the ship, where he spent the next two hours supervising the unloading and construction of the Midway by Mr. Ahasuerus' robotic crew.

There were six booths containing games of chance, two food concession stands, a gift stand, a specialty tent for Monk and the Dancer, and a tent for the strip show. He had wanted rides as well, but the Corporation had decided that the mere act of hiring a bunch of beings who weren't even members of the Community of Worlds was financial risk enough. The rides would come out of the show's profits, if any.

Flint didn't have to be an accountant to know that the next profitable world would be the first one. He was good at his job, no question about it—that was, after all, why he had been able to form a partnership with Mr. Ahasuerus and convince the distant Corporation to fund his tour—but nothing he had encountered on Earth had prepared him for the problems involved in taking his show on the galactic road.

The first planet they had played was Domar, a nondescript little world circling a nondescript little star known as Beta Scuti. The Domarians were, for the most part, a friendly and outgoing race that appeared likely to enjoy just the kind of entertainment his carnival was capable of providing. Furthermore, they were telepaths, which meant that his barkers wouldn't even need the translating devices the Corporation had furnished. It was an exciting prospect, setting up shop on his first new world, and he had anticipated a happy, prosperous, and wonder-filled two-week stand.

They were run off the planet in seven hours, and Flint had to explain to Mr. Ahasuerus, in no uncertain terms, that if his advance men *ever* booked the carnival, with its crooked games and phony patter, onto another telepathic world, there was going to be one less partner left alive to share the eventual profits.

The second world was Baaskarda. The natives seemed interested in all aspects of the carnival, they squandered their money on overpriced treats and treasures and played the games with abandon, and Flint felt in his bones that *this* world would more than make up for the first one.

They were thrown off the planet in eleven hours, barely escaping with their lives. Apparently Bruno the Bear, the star of Monk's four-animal stable, resembled the Baaskardans a little too closely, and the moment Monk started cracking his whip at Bruno a riot ensued.

By the time they reached Kligor, the third world on the tour, Fling had thoroughly checked out the physiques as well as the mental gifts of the natives, and couldn't see any reason why the carnival shouldn't finally start making a little money.

That was just what it made: a *little* money.

The Kligorites crowded into the tent to watch Monk and the Dancer in rapt fascination, and fell everlastingly in love with cotton candy and hot dogs. But their religion was based—in a way Flint never quite understood—on the principles of gambling, and the games of the Midway were just too tame compared to what they could get in church.

By the time they hit Corff, the fourth world, Flint was

learning to improvise. The local gendarmes had come by for their payoff—*some* customs remained the same the galaxy over—and Flint discovered that nothing he was doing was illegal, which made for some very unhappy policemen (or police*things*, as Flint mentally classified them). Finally he found out that it was against the laws of Corff to wear the color red. While Mr. Ahasuerus was puzzling over the social and religious causes for this, Flint dressed two of his strippers in red gowns, paraded them by the cops, paid the latter to look the other way, and everyone was happy. Unfortunately, the crowds seemed more interested in gaping at the red outfits for free than paying money to see any of the shows, and the carny took another bath—also red—but at least he felt he was finally starting to adjust to things.

Indeed, he reflected wryly, if he lived long enough he might even show a profit on one of these little jerkwater worlds.

Like this one, for instance. Name: Ramanos. Location: fifth planet circling the class G-3 star known as Tau Beta. Dominant race: the Borgraves, reasonably humanoid in appearance if you could get past those ridiculous white feathers and the webbed hands and feet. Not a member of the Community of Worlds, but aware of its existence.

Flint didn't know what they used for money, but that wasn't his department: he freely admitted to never having seen a French franc, a British pound, or a Japanese yen, and he left it up to Mr. Ahasuerus, who seemed to have literally thousands of currency conversion tables at his fingertips, to decide how much to charge for the carnival's various attractions.

Jason Diggs, a compulsive gambler and card shark who had earned the sobriquet Digger the Rigger as the kingpin of the carnival's games, had been monitoring the Borgraves' video programs for the past two days and had finally decided which games to set up in the booths. Flint noted with approval that three of them—Fascination, the Bozo, and the Loopstick—required the Borgraves to throw objects with some accuracy, which was going to prove difficult, considering their oddly webbed hands.

He wished that he had a freak show to go with the other features. He'd had one recently—a very unwilling one, which had led to his partnership with Mr. Ahasuerus—and he was firmly convinced that nothing, not even the strippers, could draw dollar-for-dollar against a truly sensational display of freaks. He'd proved that twice in the past, once with a bunch of hopeful actors in makeup, more recently with the alien tourists that Mr. Ahasuerus had shepherded to Earth.

Besides, he needed *something*. The food stands would never break even trying to sell ice cream to aliens. Monk's animals were a little less exotic in their current setting than on Earth—and sooner or later they were going to die, with no hope of replacing them. Gambling seemed to be of universal interest, but the Rigger's games were designed for humans— and Northeastern American humans at that—and it was going to take quite a while before he could devise a guaranteed moneymaker and incorporate it into the Midway. Billybuck Dancer could always attract a crowd—but just how long could anyone, even aliens who had never seen a pistol before, watch his displays of marksmanship before they got bored? After all, he never missed. Maybe if he occasionally *wounded* one of the girls . . .

Flint considered it for a moment, then shook his head. They had a limited supply of women, and he had better uses for them.

Which brought him, circuitously, back to the strip show. Of all the carnival's attractions, it was the only one that was truly unique—Mr. Ahasuerus had told him that no other planet in the galaxy had discovered the art of the striptease— and the one he had counted upon to keep the show's financial head above water while he was learning the ropes. And yet, of all the draws on the Midway, it had consistently been the poorest. Anything that ran contrary to his experience upset him, and it was Flint's experience that come good times or bad, strict towns or wide-open, tame shows or raw, sex sold.

"Tojo!" he called out suddenly.

A small hunchbacked man, perhaps thirty years old, with straight black hair and a slightly yellow cast to his skin, looked up from a tent stake he was securing.

"Yes, Thaddeus?" he stammered.

"Come here a minute. I want to talk to you."

8

The hunchback finished tying a line to the stake, stood up, and walked over to Flint with an ungainly shuffle.

"What is it, Thaddeus?"

"I think we're going to make a couple of changes tonight," said Flint, lighting a cigarette and offering one to the hunchback, who refused it.

"It's my barking, isn't it?"

"What are you talking about?"

"The way I talk," said Tojo unhappily. "The way I"—he fought to force the words out—"the way I stammer. I'm not blind, Thaddeus. I've seen the size of the crowds."

"You want to hand in your notice now, or do you think I can get in a word first?" said Flint irritably. "For a guy who keeps tripping over his tongue, you are the talkiest son of a bitch I ever met."

"I'm sorry, Thaddeus," said Tojo. "Go ahead."

"Thank you," said Fling ironically. "First, let's get one thing straight: whatever's wrong with the meat show, it's not your fault. You've got a translating device that hides your stammer, and while you're not half the barker I am, no one else is either, and that never stopped other girl shows from making money. So the problem lies somewhere else." He paused. "Is Priscilla staying off the stuff?"

"You drank it all, Thaddeus," said Tojo.

"I *know* I drank it all!" snapped Flint. "You don't have to tell me I drank it all! It was probably the best damned thing that ever happened to her, except maybe for spending a night in the sack with me. Is she getting it anywhere else?"

"Whiskey or sex?" asked Tojo.

"Whiskey, you ugly little wart!"

"No, Thaddeus, she's not getting whiskey anywhere else."

"And her act is as good as ever?"

"Her act was *never* very good."

"I've been thinking about that," admitted Flint. "Starting tonight, let Gloria lead it off."

"But she's the headliner," said Tojo.

"But nobody's going to stay to see the headliner if Priscilla chases them all out of the tent, are they?"

"I don't know if that's a good idea, Thaddeus."

9

"I don't recall asking your opinion," replied Flint. "Just tell Gloria that she's up first."

"I'll tell her," said Tojo with a sigh. "But I wish you'd stop by and listen to my patter. I still think *I'm* the problem."

"It's not you," said Flint, a little more gently. He took a deep drag on his cigarette. "You worked with me every night for six years. Some of that talent couldn't help but rub off."

"Still . . ." persisted Tojo.

"All right! Just tell Gloria she's up to bat first, and I promise to come by and check you out."

"Thank you, Thaddeus," said Tojo, walking back to the tent and securing yet another rope to one of the corner stakes. Flint watched the little hunchback throw himself into his work, whistling the score of some Broadway show or other so he wouldn't embarrass himself by tripping over the words. At least, reflected Flint with a sardonic smile, *someone* was adjusting to things without much difficulty.

The rest of the afternoon was devoted to printing tickets (different worlds with different currencies required different tickets, another minor problem that had never occurred to him until it became a major one). Swede returned about thirty minutes before sunset with the observation that these marks didn't seem any stranger than any of the others, which Flint tried without much enthusiasm to view in a positive manner. Then the sun was gone, three moons slowly clambered up over the horizon, Flint gave the signal, and the Midway was bathed in thousands of colored lights. He walked to the control tent, inserted a cassette of calliope music into a recorder, hooked it in to the sound system—and the carnival was open for business.

As he walked out to greet those few Borgraves who had arrived ahead of what he hoped would be the huge crowd from the city, Monk pulled him aside and informed him that the leopards simply couldn't get the hang of this world's gravity, and that he was going to have to go with just Simba and Bruno, which meant that the Dancer would have to add some fifteen to twenty minutes to his act. Flint nodded, and told him to inform Mr. Ahasuerus and the Dancer of the problem.

Then he began checking out the games, and realized that

the Rigger was in for a long night: the Borgraves' hands were so misshapen that most of them couldn't even pick up a ball or a hoop, let alone throw them accurately, and *that* in turn meant that only three of the six games were going to take in any money to speak of. He started thinking very fondly of the little towns in Maine and Vermont that he had abandoned to seek his fortune amid the glittering, mysterious stars. At least the marks of Earth were a little more predictable, a little more familiar, and it was a rare evening that some local girl didn't try to convince him, in her own inimitable manner, that she was just what he needed for the meat show. . . .

A few hundred more Borgraves filtered in, and then he remembered the strip show, and walked over to check it out.

He stepped inside the tent and stood at the back as Tojo, dressed in a candy-striped coat, white pants, and a straw boater, stood atop a box that was mounted on the side of the stage and spoke into his translating device. He wondered if the little hunchback knew how silly he looked, like some misshapen monkey mocking a human being, then shrugged as he decided that Tojo probably didn't look any sillier to the audience than he himself did.

He became aware of a strange birdlike sound permeating the tent, and realized that it was coming from the translator. Annoyed—the pitch of the sound hurt his ears—he walked to the side of the tent and approached the stage so that he could hear Tojo's untranslated patter as he spoke into the mechanism.

". . . the Toast of a Thousand Worlds," cried the little hunchback, "the most sexciting ecdysiast in the civilized universe, a frothy feline morsel who's got curves in places where most girls don't even have places . . ."

On and on he droned as Flint caught his eye and nodded in approval and Tojo smiled back in obvious relief. Flint recognized most of the lines as having been lifted from his own patter back on Earth, and wondered what the mechanism was doing with the alliteration and the phony come-on words such as "sexciting."

Tojo kept speaking until the tent was full, then uttered a cue phrase. Someone backstage hit a switch, and a recording of "Harlem Nocturne" was piped into the tent.

"All right, ladies and gentlemen," said Tojo, climbing off

11

his box and carrying it to the edge of the stage. "Here's the moment you've all been waiting for. Here she is, boys; here she is, world; here she is, galaxy! Here's *Butterfly Delight!*"

Tojo clambered off the stage, the rhythm of the recording picked up steam, and then, from behind a curtain, stepped Gloria Stunkel, all feathers and beads and sequins and satin. She pursed her bright-red lips, creating soundless little explosions in time with the insistent beat of the snare drum, and undulated to the center of the stage.

"How did I do, Thaddeus?" asked Tojo, walking over to join him.

"Just fine," replied Flint, his eyes never leaving the girl on the stage.

"You're sure?" persisted Tojo.

"I couldn't have done better myself," lied Flint. "You're such a lecherous little bastard to begin with . . ." He snorted. "I just hope you didn't get them so turned on that Gloria can't deliver."

That seemed to satisfy Tojo, and Flint returned his attention to the stage.

Gloria had removed a shoulder-length glove and was in the process of slithering out of her gown. It fell to the stage in a heap, and she kicked it into the wings with an eye-popping bump.

Six Borgraves walked out of the tent.

Gloria started grinding her hips, punctuating the motion with bumps to match the drumbeat, then unhooked her bra and spent about twenty seconds teasing the audience, flashing her breasts at them, before removing it and tossing it after the gown.

Four more Borgraves left.

Gloria's pasties had glittery tassels, and she began rotating them, first clockwise, then counterclockwise, then in opposite directions. They began moving so fast that Flint half-thought she might take off like a helicopter.

Eleven more Borgraves made their way to the exit.

Gloria stripped down to her G-string, threw her pasties to the crowd—which ducked—and lowered herself to the floor, where she commenced a series of sensuous gyrations.

Flint studied her with an expert eye. This wasn't the kind

12

of show Ann Corio was putting on for middle-aged house-wives who wondered what their husbands had been so inter-ested in twenty or thirty years ago, but it wasn't strong, either—at least, not *carny* strong. And he had to admit she was damned good at her job.

Then she was on her feet again, shaking, bumping, swaying, pulsating, fantasizing with the curtains, contorting her sweat-ing body in ways that no one who hadn't seen her perform would ever have believed possible.

Twenty Borgraves left.

Flint became aware of an insistent tugging at his sleeve.

"Thaddeus, she's dying up there!" whispered Tojo halt-ingly. "You've got to do something."

"Like what—lock the doors?"

"She's a *star*, Thaddeus," persisted Tojo. "You can't let this happen to her."

"All right," said Flint with a sigh. "Have you got that translator?"

Tojo unhooked the mechanism from his collar and handed it to Flint.

"Let's get to the back of the tent, where she can't hear me speak into it." A moment later he had posted himself in the doorway. "How do you turn this damned thing on?"

Tojo pointed to the switch, and Flint activated it.

"Borgraves!" he shouted into the translating device. "This is one of the holiest and most sacred rituals of my race. Please do not offend our practitioner by walking out or otherwise distracting her. Your money will be refunded at the conclusion of the performance."

Most of the Borgraves continued leaving, but a few hesi-tated and returned to their seats as Flint repeated his message twice more.

"Satisfied?" he said, handing the mechanism back to Tojo.

"What happened, Thaddeus?" asked Tojo. "Why did they all leave?"

"You know," said Flint thoughtfully, "I think I've finally got a handle on this problem."

"What is it?"

"Would *you* pay good money to watch a bird molting to music?" replied Flint with a rueful grin.

Gloria was finishing her act, her sultry animation replaced by a frozen mannequin's smile, her movements still correct but now mechanical, her eyes puzzled and hurt. The music clicked off and she struck a final pose, the same one that had drawn wild ovations from thousands of appreciative audiences on Earth.

The seventeen remaining Borgraves walked out without a sound.

Flint and Tojo sat alone in the back of the tent in silence. Finally Flint lit a cigarette.

"Tojo, starting tomorrow I want you to move over and bark for Monk and the Dancer."

"What about the strip show?"

"I'm shutting it down."

"You're sure?"

Flint nodded. "Maybe running the only meat show in the galaxy wasn't as bright an idea as I thought." He shook his head. "Oh, well. Tell the girls to report to the Rigger in the morning."

"All right," said Tojo uncomfortably.

"What's the matter?"

"Well, Priscilla and Barbara will probably be overjoyed. They never gave a damn about stripping. But Gloria . . ."

"I know," said Flint. "Tell you what. You talk to the other two, and I'll speak to Gloria myself."

"Thank you, Thaddeus," said Tojo, looking much relieved.

"Let's give her a few minutes to calm down first," said Flint. He put his feet on the chair ahead of him, finished his cigarette in silence, then got up and walked over to Gloria's makeshift backstage dressing room.

He could tell by the streaks in her makeup that she had been crying, and he was glad he hadn't arrived any sooner. Now she just looked puzzled as she sat before her mirror.

"What did I do wrong, Thaddeus?" she asked when she became aware of his presence.

"Nothing," he said gently.

"But they all walked out! You saw them. I mean, it's been bad on other worlds, but this is the worst. Is it *me?*"

"It's not you. It's just the nature of the beast."

"I don't understand."

14

"What I'm trying to say is that aliens have about as much interest in your body as you have in theirs." He paused for a moment, trying to figure out how to soften the blow, couldn't see any way, and just came out with it: "I'm closing down the strip show."

Gloria looked her dismay. "You can't!"

"I can't afford to keep it open."

"But what will I do?" she said plaintively. "Where will I go? Stripping is the only thing I know!"

"You'll stay with us, and you'll learn how to do something else," replied Flint, pulling a flask out of his pocket and unscrewing the top. "Here. Take a sip. You'll feel better."

"I don't want a sip, and I don't want to do anything else!" she said, fighting back her tears. "I've been a stripper all my life. I *like* being on stage, I *like* making people happy, I *like* what I do. I'm not like the other girls in the show, Thaddeus— you know that. I work out every morning, I exercise two hours a day, I make my own costumes, I do my own choreography, I—"

"The problem isn't *you*," he said wearily. "It's *them*."

"You promised me I'd be the headliner," she said, looking at him reproachfully. "That's the reason I agreed to leave Earth—because I believed you. You *can't* shut down the show."

"You're upset now," said Flint gently. "We'll talk about it tomorrow."

She lowered her head in thought, suddenly oblivious to his presence. "Maybe it was the music. Maybe it grated on their ears. . . ."

He sighed and walked out of the tent.

Diggs was trying, without much success, to show a Borgrave family how to pick up and hold a rubber ball, and Jenny and Lori, two of the other games workers, were sitting in splendid isolation within their booths, unable to attract a single customer. The three remaining games were doing some business, though Flint couldn't tell if it was enough to break even. The Dancer had filled the specialty tent—but the Dancer *always* filled the specialty tent. He heard a deep bellowing curse, stared off into the darkness, and saw that Monk was still trying unsuccessfully to get his leopards to adjust to Ramanos' gravity. Swede was working the food stand, futilely explaining the joys of coffee and soda pop to a trio of dubious Borgraves. And, Flint was sure, Gloria was still convincing herself that the reason the crowd had walked out had to do with the sound of the music or the intensity of the lights or the shape of the chairs.

He looked up at the night sky and wondered wistfully how business was in Vermont.

3.

An iguana would have been right at home on Procyon III. A transplanted scorpion would never have known that it wasn't still on a desert back on Earth. Even Flint was having trouble distinguishing this world from the last five, and secretly wondered if the Community of Worlds really amounted to anything more than a bunch of galactic backwoods provinces.

The Ahasuerus and Flint Traveling Carnival and Sideshow had played Ramanos for five days of a projected fourteen-day tour, then packed up and moved over to Procyon, some seven light-years away, with their record still intact: they had now gone through five worlds without once showing a profit.

Flint was sitting on the sand, propped up against a small termite hill (or, rather, the Procyonian equivalent of a termite hill), looking out at the vast expanse of desert and wondering how soon his supply of beer would be gone if he kept drinking it at his current rate, when he noticed his partner approaching him.

"I've revised my opinion," he announced.

"About what?" asked Mr. Ahasuerus.

"About how long it's going to take Man to conquer the galaxy once he figures out how to travel to the stars." Flint took a long swallow of his beer and wiped his mouth off with a sweaty shirtsleeve. "I give us three weeks, tops." He

17

paused again. "That's twenty days to decide whether it's worth the effort, and one afternoon to pull it off."

"Am I to assume you are unimpressed with Procyon III?" inquired Mr. Ahasuerus mildly.

"I'd say that's a pretty fair assumption," replied Flint. "Granting that we are not playing the most sophisticated worlds on the circuit to begin with, why the hell do we always have to land thirty miles or more from the nearest goddamned city?"

"Most of these planets don't have spaceports," the blue man pointed out.

"I know. But why not five or ten miles?"

"Regulations."

"Well," sighed Flint. "I've got to admit that's one place where you're ahead of us. I have the feeling my bureaucracy could learn one hell of a lot from your bureaucracy." He finished his beer and threw the can out onto the sand, where it rolled for twelve or fifteen yards before coming to a halt. "How the hell do you pick these worlds?"

"It's part of the circuit. We could change the order, if you wish."

Flint shook his head. "A cesspool is going to be a cesspool whether we visit it first or tenth."

"Procyon III *does* have a gravity identical to Earth's," said Mr. Ahasuerus apologetically.

"I suspect that it's also about as heavily populated as Saskatchewan."

"I am unacquainted with that location," said the blue man.

"So is everyone else." Suddenly Flint looked up. "You didn't come out here just to listen to me bitch. What's up? Is one of the animals sick?"

The blue man shook his head.

"I have had a communication from the Corporation," he said.

"And?"

"They are, of course, concerned about our lack of success."

"Tell them these things take a while. I ran in the red the first two years I had the show back on Earth."

"I told them so," replied Mr. Ahasuerus, looking decidedly uncomfortable.

18

"They'd better not be thinking of closing us down!" said Flint ominously. "Because if they are, I've got a contract."

"That eventuality never came up," said the blue man. "But . . ."

"But what?"

"They are sending an efficiency expert out here to examine our operation."

"In a pig's asshole they are!" exploded Flint, leaping to his feet. "That's just what I need—some hotshot junior executive who's never seen a carny, trying to score brownie points with the Corporation by telling us how to run one!"

"Calm down, Mr. Flint."

"Up yours, Mr. Ahasuerus! You get on the radio and tell the boy wonder that I'm not letting him set foot on the grounds."

"I really don't see how we can stop him," said Mr. Ahasuerus.

"You watch me!" snarled Flint. "Your fucking Corporation's got five thousand businesses on six hundred worlds. They're rich enough to carry us until we find out what combinations click."

"They didn't get rich by not attending to details, Mr. Flint," the blue man pointed out mildly.

"Look—you get them on the radio and tell them that Thaddeus Flint says he's getting seriously displeased with them!"

"I think the feeling may be mutual," said Mr. Ahasuerus wryly. "Let us make the best of the situation."

"We aren't going to *have* a situation if he keeps away," said Flint.

The blue man sighed deeply. "Mr. Flint, I have been an employee of the Corporation for well over thirty years. Please don't jeopardize my position by causing a scene over a problem that is beyond my power to alleviate."

Flint stared at him for a long moment. "I'm sorry," he said at last. "Let me know when he's due to arrive, and I'll see what we can work out."

"Thank you, Mr. Flint."

"You wouldn't believe how unwelcome you are, Mr. Ahasuerus," replied Flint.

19

He walked the blue man back to the Midway, which had been erected that morning, and sought out a chair that was shaded by the overhang of one of the game booths.

It was, he had to admit, a pretty poor excuse for a carnival. No rides, only six game booths, no meat show, no freak show. He knew the real reason he didn't want anyone from the Corporation snooping around, and it had nothing to do with infringing on his prerogatives: the man (or thing, or whatever) would take one look and start trying to find ways to break Flint's contract.

And yet, there *was* money to be made on these damned dirtballs, if he could just figure out how to spring it loose. Maybe he should be staying three or four months on each planet, learning more about the natives, rather than trying this scattershot approach . . . but four months on any of these worlds would drive him up a tree quicker than four years in Newark, New Jersey. They just didn't come up to his preconceived notion of a galactic civilization.

"Got a minute?" said a familiar voice, and Flint turned to face Jason Diggs, who, despite the fact that showtime was still hours off, was decked out in his usual natty garb: derby hat, white shirt, black bowtie, red vest, red garters on his sleeves, brightly checked slacks, and black patent-leather shoes.

"Have a seat," said Flint, indicating an empty chair next to him.

The Rigger sat down and lit a small, thin cigar.

"Hot," he commented.

"So loosen your tie."

Diggs shook his head. "Start letting yourself go on these jerkwater worlds, and pretty soon you're four hundred pounds and shacking up with a lady lizard."

Flint shrugged. "Suit yourself. How are the girls working out?"

"Well, considering that you never hired them for their brainpower, I'd say they're doing okay. I've got Barbara working the shell game, and Priscilla's on the Fascination booth."

"And Gloria?"

"She still won't report to work. I saw her practicing her

belly dancing this morning." He shook his head. "For a sexy broad, she's the most awkward goddamned dancer I ever saw."

"I know."

"How come she's such a good stripper?"

"Vulnerability," replied Flint. "In stripping, it translates as just enough shyness or awkwardness to make the audience think she hasn't done her routine ten thousand times before."

"You going to let her belly dance?"

"What am I supposed to do: walk up and tell her she's got two left feet?"

"They'll laugh at her, Thaddeus."

"No they won't. They've never seen a *good* belly dancer. They'll walk out on her, just like they do when she strips."

"How long are you going to let this go on?"

"Until she gets tired of it."

"What makes you think she will?" asked the Rigger.

"Sooner or later she'd got to. Even Stogie gave up after a while."

Stogie was Max Bloom, the ancient baggy-pants comic.

"There's a difference," Diggs pointed out. "Stogie never thought what he was doing was an art form. He told three dirty jokes to that race that reproduces by budding—what were they called? The Kligorites—and knew he'd had it. My biggest problem now is that he wants to work the Bozo cage."

Flint grimaced. "That's just what we need: a seventy-one-year-old clown getting dunked in cold water fifty times a night with no doctor around. He wouldn't live out the week."

"You know it and I know it, and probably *he* knows it too, but he says he's too old to learn a new routine."

"And getting dunked is an *old* routine?"

"No," said Diggs. "But insulting the customers is. And that's what the Bozo is supposed to do: get 'em so mad they pay for the balls and try to knock him off his perch."

"Out of the question," said Flint.

"That's what I keep telling him, but he's pretty adamant."

"What's the platform—about three feet above the water?" asked Flint. "Hell, the fall would probably kill him. Besides, I really wonder if we shouldn't leave the Bozo booth in mothballs. Maybe one of these nights our Bozo will holler out the wrong insult and we'll have a war on our hands.''

"Am I wrong,'' remarked the Rigger, "or are you a little more irritable than usual?''

"The Corporation is sending someone to check out the operation.''

"Ahhh!'' said Diggs. "Well, we'll just have to flim-flam him.''

"Or *some*body.''

"You want us to start gaffing?'' asked Diggs. "I thought we were supposed to be playing it straight.''

"I wanted to, I really did,'' replied Flint. "But I've got to show this guy that we've turned the corner and started making a profit or there's no telling what kind of a hassle he'll give us.''

"What'll your partner say?''

"He'll say: no crooked games—but there's more than one way to skin a cat.''

"You got something particular in mind?''

"Yeah. Teach Barbara how to work a Skillo game, and you set up a Psychic booth.''

The Rigger guffawed. "A Psychic booth! Lord, I haven't worked one of those for twenty years. Everyone got wise to them after a while.''

"We're not going to be here that long,'' replied Flint. "We'll run it as long as it keeps the marks happy, and then we'll switch to an Auction.''

"My oh my!'' grinned the Rigger. "You really *do* want to make a buck, don't you?''

"It might be a pleasant change,'' commented Flint dryly. "And make sure Tojo and Stogie are watching you tonight, so they can learn how it works.''

"There's nothing to it,'' chuckled Diggs. "The trick is just not to be too smart.''

"Then we *all* ought to be experts. Have you got enough slum?''

"Probably not.''

"Then get some money from Mr. Ahasuerus and take the landcar into town and pick up what you need.''

"Right,'' said the Rigger. "I'll be back in two hours.''

22

"Remember to take a translator!" Flint called after him.

He suddenly realized that he hadn't eaten all day—the five beers didn't really count—so he went to the ship's mess hall for a sandwich. Gloria was sitting there, drinking some concoction of fruit juices and reading a paperback romance novel she'd brought along from Earth.

"How's it going?" Flint asked pleasantly, taking a seat at her table and unwrapping his sandwich.

"The Rigger thinks I'm not very good," she replied, looking up from her book.

"Are you?"

"I will be," she said stubbornly.

Flint shrugged. "Then don't listen to him."

"He didn't say anything. But I could tell from the expression on his face."

"Have you given any thought to what you're going to use for music?" he inquired. "All we have on tape are snare drums and calliopes."

"I'll come up with something. Finger cymbals, maybe."

"I didn't know you had any."

"I don't—but I can have one of Ahasuerus' robots make some. After all, they do anything except set the show up and break it down. They've got lots of time."

"They're *programmed* to assemble and disassemble tents and booths. I don't know if they can make finger cymbals."

"Then I'll use something else!" she snapped. "Don't you start in on me too, Thaddeus! I've had enough of that for one week."

"Oh? From who?"

"Barbara and Priscilla."

"What did they say?"

"They keep trying to convince me that stripping is degrading." She snorted contemptuously. "I notice they didn't think so as long as they could make money at it. Besides, I'd like to know what's so goddamned uplifting about shilling for the Rigger!"

"Calm down," said Flint. "You don't have to work the games unless you want to."

"I know," she said more gently. "It's just so frustrating!

23

In my whole life I've only been able to do one thing well, and now no one wants me to do it!''

"It's not a matter of what *we* want. It's a matter of what the marks will pay for."

"That's why I'm working on my belly dancing."

"And if they don't pay for that either?" he asked mildly.

"Then I'll think of something else. One way or another I'm going to find a way to make audiences happy."

"I'll settle for just making them poorer," he said wryly.

"You don't think I can do it!" she said hotly, rising from the table. "Well, you'll see!"

She walked out the airlock, and Flint turned to watch her. There was a certain sexy swing to her buttocks, no question about it, and she swayed and jiggled just like the girls on the TV shows back on Earth, but the very things that made her look so delectable—her posture, the way she set her feet down so heavily—would work against her as a dancer. Stripping mimicked the sweaty gyrations of the sex act, and a degree of awkwardness made both stripping and sex all the more enticing. But dancing, and especially belly dancing, was an athletic discipline: the belly fluttered instead of bumping, the hips shimmied instead of grinding, the floorwork put pressure on muscles she hadn't used in years.

Still, if it made her happy to try, why not? At least when she finally went to work in the booths she wouldn't blame him for not giving her every chance to remain a performer. And besides, it wasn't as if the game booths were being overrun with customers these days.

He was still staring at the airlock when Mr. Ahasuerus entered the ship and walked over to him.

"I have just given Diggs three hundred credits to go into town and buy some slum," announced the blue man.

"Good. How much is a credit worth?"

"On Procyon III, it will buy the equivalent of eighty cents American."

"That'll be enough," said Flint. "And if it isn't, we can always get more."

"Then, since this meets with your approval, perhaps you can tell me, just for the record, what *slum* is? I had the obviously mistaken impression that it referred to decrepit tenement buildings.''

Flint chuckled. "It's carny slang. The Rigger is off hunting up a few gross of very cheap gifts at a wholesale house in town.''

"Which wholesale house?''

"How the hell do I know? I've only been on the goddamned planet for five or six hours.''

"I wish you would come to me with your needs,'' said Mr. Ahasuerus patiently. "The Corporation owns a number of businesses on Procyon III. Even if they couldn't supply us with what we need, we could surely use their discounts.''

"Believe me, Mr. Ahasuerus,'' replied Flint, "if I had sent anyone but Diggs I would have cleared it with you first.''

"What makes him different?''

"I saw a couple of bulges in his vest pocket,'' said Flint with a smile. "I would imagine that right about now he is giving some poor Procyonian warehouse owner a quick course in how to shoot craps, which will be followed by an even quicker course in the statistical redistribution of Procyonian wealth.''

"With our luck, it will be a Corporation warehouse,'' commented the blue man.

"I never even thought of that,'' admitted Flint.

"Just out of curiosity, why do we have to purchase more gifts?'' asked Mr. Ahasuerus. "I should have thought that was the one commodity with which we were adequately supplied, especially in light of the business we've been doing.''

"Oh, we've got a lot of gifts lying around the ship, that's for sure,'' said Flint. "But some of them are a little too good. Slum are really cheap gifts, the kind of things we pick up for two or three cents apiece in quantity.''

"And we need them?''

"Don't let it upset you,'' replied Flint. "If things go right, we won't have any left by tomorrow morning.''

"You intend to give them all away tonight?''

"Not exactly.''

"Then what?''

"Stop by the Rigger's booth tonight and see for yourself.''

"I will. And if you and Mr. Diggs are conspiring to run a crooked game . . ."

"Partner, you cut me to the quick!" grinned Flint.

Mr. Ahasuerus stared at him for a moment, then walked to the private elevator that would take him to his office on the top level of the ship.

Flint finished his sandwich, had another, washed it down with his sixth beer of the day, and spent the next couple of hours strolling around the Midway, checking out the booths, making sure Monk's animals were adapting to the planet, trying unsuccessfully to get the Dancer to practice, and getting another brief but spellbinding demonstration that further practice was unnecessary. He saw Priscilla diligently trying to raise Gloria's consciousness and gave the pair of them a wide berth, then went back to his room aboard ship for a nap.

When he awoke the sun was just setting, and Diggs had returned from town bearing two dozen cartons of odd little artifacts: cheap jewelry, rag figures that seemed to be the Procyonian equivalent of dolls, and a number of glittery, strangely shaped metallic objects for which he could discern no purpose.

A fair-sized opening-night crowd began arriving at sunset, and Flint estimated that better than three thousand Procyonians would pass through the Midway that night. It wasn't much compared to some of the business he'd done on Earth, but then, with no rides or girl show or freak show, this wasn't much of a carnival compared to the one he'd had on Earth either, and he was in no position to look a gift horse in the mouth—not even a very small gift horse.

Mr. Ahasuerus joined him a few minutes after dark, and they walked over to the Psychic booth. Diggs was sitting on a stool, telling jokes that none of the Procyonians understood while waiting for the crowd to build a little more, and doing enough card tricks to guarantee that no human who saw him would ever get into a poker or blackjack game with him. As his patter and routine continued he began getting just a little too pompous, a little too ostentatious about his skill with cards, and the crowd started getting hostile.

"You'd better tell him to modify his pitch," said Mr. Ahasuerus softly.

"He's got a reason," answered Flint.

"You mean he *wants* them mad at him?"

Flint nodded. "Watch," he whispered.

Diggs kept on speaking for another five minutes, then put his cards away and hooked up a microphone to his translator.

"All right," he announced. "It's show time. I'm all through showing you how dumb you are." He checked his watch. "It's eight o'clock now"—the time, as well as the language, was translated into Procyonian terms—"and I'm so goddamned sure of myself I promise that I'm not going to get out of this booth until midnight." He gestured to the slum. "You see these gifts? Well, ordinarily we limit them one to a customer, but your brains are so goddamned easy for me to read that I'm going to give each of you a present for every single question I can't answer." He suddenly pointed to a male at the back of the crowd. "I read that thought, sir, and all I can say is: the same to you!"

He looked around until he spotted Tojo. "Tojo, my good man, go out among these clods and start collecting money. One credit per question; no more, no less." He paused to clear his throat. "This is how it works, bumpkins. You ask me any question you like: how far it is to Sigma Alpha, whose house you robbed last night, anything at all. If I answer it correctly, as I'm sure to do, you pay me double—two credits. If I'm wrong, which happens about once every five years, and then only when I've been drinking, you can have any one of these beautiful presents."

He looked out at the crowd. "Are we ready to begin?"

"Do these guys know we're not telepaths?" whispered Flint.

"Yes," replied the blue man.

Flint smiled. "Duck soup," he commented.

A male in the front of the crowd gave Tojo a credit.

"What my name?" he asked.

Diggs looked long and hard at him. "George Washington Carver," he announced at last.

The male gave the Procyonian equivalent of a raspberry, and showed an identification tag to Diggs. The Rigger couldn't read a word of it, but he glared at it as if he couldn't believe

27

it, then shrugged and gestured to the gifts. The Procyonian took one, then asked Diggs to name his address.

"One question to a customer!" roared the Rigger.

The crowd started screaming that he had made no such precondition, so Diggs sighed and went to work. Within five minutes he had guessed that the Procyonian lived at 121 Broadway in Manhattan, worked for the New York Yankees, had eaten scrambled eggs for breakfast, and had come to the carnival in a 1978 Ford Mustang. All, of course, were wrong.

"Enough's enough!" bellowed Diggs, getting red in the face. "Is it *my* fault this creature is too goddamned stupid to have a mind to read? Someone else ask me something. Fair is fair!"

A female offered two credits to Tojo, and asked Diggs to name her two offsprings.

"Groucho and Harpo," was the answer.

Within another fifteen minutes he had guessed incorrectly on forty more questions, and was fit to be tied.

"That's all!" he cried. "I don't know what's wrong, but the show's over! This has never happened to me before."

A couple of huge males—Flint imagined they were the equivalent of Procyonian truckdrivers—shouldered their way to the front and reminded him that he had promised not to close the booth until midnight.

"But I'm going broke!" he wailed.

Tough, was their answer.

"Is he going to make a right answer all night?" asked Mr. Ahasuerus.

"Probably not," said Flint. "On Earth he'd probably have the bad luck to come up with a right one every twenty questions or so, but here he ought to be safe."

"*Safe?*" repeated the blue man. "But he's losing a present on every guess!"

"How much did each present cost us?"

"About two cents."

"And how much is he getting for each wrong answer?" grinned Flint.

Mr. Ahasuerus' eyes widened. "I see."

"You can't say it's a crooked game. We're giving them presents whether they want them or not, and poor Diggs is up

28

there getting humiliated in front of everyone after he started the evening by insulting them."

"There's a little more to this than meets the eye, Mr. Flint," said Mr. Ahasuerus, exposing his teeth in what passed for a smile.

"You think that's something?" laughed Flint. "Come on over and let me show you how a Skillo game works."

The blue man accompanied him to where Barbara was running the Skillo booth, which had five identical games in it. Mr. Ahasuerus watched for a few minutes as the marks tried to roll marbles into a numbered hole, then turned to Flint.

"It looks easy."

"It is."

"Then why—"

"It's easy to *win*. It's impossible to *beat*."

"I'm not sure I understand you."

"It costs five credits to play," explained Flint. "Depending on the numerical combinations, you can win one, three, ten, or a thousand credits. It's about fifty-fifty that you'll win one, and you've got a one-in-five chance of winning three. You'd have to play an average of fifty games before you'd win ten."

"And a thousand?"

"A mathematician I knew in Florida worked it out once," said Flint with a smile. "He said it was a . . . I can't remember the term, but he had a funny-sounding name for it."

"A googol?" asked Mr. Ahasuerus.

"That was it! A googol-to-one against. How much is a googol?"

"Ten to the one hundredth power."

"Anyway, we aren't real likely to have to pay off."

"And why are you bringing out these games now, Mr. Flint?" asked Mr. Ahasuerus.

"To show your friend from the Corporation that we can turn a profit if we have to."

"I must have expressed myself poorly," said the blue man. "What I meant was, why haven't we been running these games all along?"

"Because the night we formed our partnership, all I heard from you and the Corporation was how I had to run a totally legit show." He paused to light a cigarette, another of his rapidly vanishing commodities. "The thing is, what I'm good at is bilking marks. It's what I've done my whole life. We're going to make eight thousand credits tonight just off the Psychic and Skillo booths, and look around you—the whole damned crew is feeling sharp again. We're doing what we know how to do."

"As long as the games aren't out-and-out crooked, I see no reason why they shouldn't be considered legitimate," said the blue man. "You should have discussed this with me earlier."

"The timing was wrong."

"I beg your pardon?"

"We weren't going broke earlier. Would you really have agreed to a Skillo game on the first couple of worlds?"

"Perhaps not," admitted the blue man. "And I must confess that I would have been wrong."

Flint chuckled. "We'll make a Man out of you yet, Mr. Ahasuerus."

"Fate forfend, Mr. Flint."

Flint left his partner and made a tour of the Midway. The Dancer's show—full, as always—was just letting out, and there was already a moderate crowd lined up to see Monk and his animals. Diggs was taking in money faster than he could count it, and sardonically signaled to Flint that he had inadvertently guessed right on four questions thus far. Priscilla's Fascination booth was at least breaking even, and Jenny and Lori were actually turning a profit. Only Gloria, rigged out in a costume that was halfway between a stripper's gown and a harem outfit, had failed to draw a crowd, despite the fact that she had Stogie barking for her and the old comic was practically dragging reluctant customers into her small tent.

"Forty-six hundred credits, Thaddeus," said Tojo, when the carnival had closed for the night. "That's some scam, that Psychic game. "I've never seen it before."

"It takes someone like the Rigger to pull it off," remarked Flint. "Most of the marks figure out after a half hour or so that he's never going to come up with a right answer and that they're getting nothing but slum for their money, but if you

30

can get 'em mad enough, make 'em want to humiliate you enough, you can keep the thing going all night.''

"I hear the Skillo game took in almost three thousand credits, too," said the little hunchback.

"Yeah. I think we're going to be ready for this hotshot Corporation executive in a couple more days."

"I heard about him. Can he really cause us any trouble?''

"Not as much as I can cause him," said Flint. "If those bastards really gave a damn about us, they'd keep their efficiency expert and send us a decent advance man. This world's okay, but one in six isn't much of a percentage."

"Isn't that what Fast Johnny's doing—advance work?''

"I don't know what the hell Fast Johnny's doing," said Flint irritably. "I sent him out two months ago and I haven't heard a word from him since.''

"Maybe it took him a while to recover from the operation," suggested Tojo.

"You remember what Mr. Romany told us back on Earth," said Flint. "Two weeks and out. Three at the most.''

"But look what they turned him into.''

"It's old hat to these people, Tojo. Making Romany look like a Man was probably every bit as hard as making Fast Johnny into a—well, whatever the hell he is now. It makes sense, I suppose—meeting the natives of a new world not just on their own turf but in their own image as well. I just hope the son of a bitch hasn't gone native on us.''

"As a six-foot-long gray slug?" said Tojo dubiously.

Flint laughed. "It's a pretty stupid notion at that." He paused. "I wonder why the hell he hasn't reported in?''

4.

John Edward Carp undulated across the moist brown vegetation, sniffing colors, tasting sounds. He had not eaten for
three days, but he felt no pangs of hunger, nor would he for
another week.

He came to a slope in the trail he had been following, and,
after considering his alternatives, elected to roll his gray,
reticulated body down to the base of it. Then, shaking himself
off, he continued slithering in the direction of his ship, content and serene.

He had only one regret in the world: that he wouldn't be
able to see the expression on Thaddeus Flint's face when he
sent in his resignation.

5.

Gloria was sitting at her vanity, her sewing kit laid out before her, meticulously reattaching a Velcro fastener that was coming loose from one of her gowns, when there was a knock at her door.

"Come in," she said, without looking up.

A moment later Tojo, dressed in a long-sleeved shirt and jeans, entered the room.

"Can I speak to you for a minute?" he stammered.

"Just a second," she replied, inserting a last stitch and then carefully hanging the gown against her closet door to stretch the wrinkles out. "Thaddeus sent you, didn't he?" she said, finally turning to the hunchback.

"He wants to know if you'd like me to teach you the Psychic routine," said Tojo.

"I thought so! Listen to me, you ugly little dwarf—you go back to your boss and tell him to get off my case! I'm a dancer, not a goddamned con artist!"

"I know," said Tojo. "I'm sorry I bothered you, but he's the boss, and . . ."

Her face softened. "I didn't mean to yell at you. It's not your fault. You look hot: can I give you something to drink?"

"That would be very nice, thank you."

She opened a small, built-in refrigerator, pulled out a pitcher, filled two glasses, and handed one to him. "It's a coconut-pineapple combination that one of the robots synthesized for me.'' He stared at it dubiously. "Go ahead, drink it. It's a lot healthier than Thaddeus' beer.''

Tojo shrugged. "When you're hot, I suppose anything tastes good.'' He took a long swallow and immediately screwed up his face as the flavor hit him.

"If you'd wear a T-shirt like everyone else, you wouldn't sweat so much,'' said Gloria.

"This fits a little more loosely,'' he replied.

"What difference does that make?'' she asked. Then her eyes fell on his hump. "Oh. I see.''

"Why make people look at something they find distasteful?'' he said.

"By the same token, we ought to lock Mr. Ahasuerus in cold storage for the rest of the tour. Don't be so sensitive, Tojo.'' She walked over to a recliner chair and sat down. "How long before Thaddeus stops *asking* me to work the games and starts *telling* me?''

The hunchback shrugged. "I really don't know. I think he's a little bit afraid of you.''

She laughed derisively. "Nothing scares Thaddeus Flint.''

"Yes, it does,'' said Tojo, placing his glass on the vanity and sitting on the chair. "He's afraid to fail. You were the only stripper we had back on Earth who refused to work strong when he gave the word, and you made it stick. He might be afraid of what will happen if he orders you to run a booth.''

"I was the only *stripper* he had at all,'' said Gloria firmly. "Where does Priscilla get off lecturing me about degrading myself, anyway? I spent years studying my craft and refining my routines. All she ever did was walk out naked on a stage and let the audience paw her. Where's the art in that, Tojo?''

"There wasn't any,'' he admitted. "But it was what the marks paid for.''

"The marks were a bunch of freaks and perverts. That doesn't mean we had to lower ourselves to their level. I'm a stripper, not a whore.''

"Whores take money,'' he pointed out gently.

"Whores make transactions: their bodies for something they want, whether it's money or a trip to the stars or good

34

treatment from the boss. I don't do that. I never did and I never will.''

"I never said you did," replied Tojo.

"Yeah? Well, *he* wanted me to."

"Thaddeus?"

"He lied to me to get me to join the carny, and he lied again to get me to come out here. First he told me he wanted a stripper, when all he really wanted was another slut to sit on the marks' faces. Then he told me we'd be playing cities that would make New York look like a hick town." She paused for breath. "Look around you, Tojo. Do *you* see any of those cities, any of those audiences he promised me? All I've seen is one dust bowl after another, and my audiences are all things with feathers or scales!''

"I'm sure he didn't know it was a lie when he said it," replied Tojo gently. "I know how much he was looking forward to coming out here. He's as disappointed as you are."

"I find that hard to believe," she said bitterly. "He's still doing what he always did—finding new ways to screw the marks. Hell, he's probably happy to have a new challenge."

"He's been a driven man all his life. Personally, I think he's tired of challenges." Tojo paused uncomfortably. "Would it be so terrible for you to help him in the booths?"

"Yes!"

"Can you help me to understand why?" continued Tojo. "I'm not asking this for *him*," he added hastily. "But it just doesn't make any sense to me. All my life I wanted to *belong* to something, to feel that I was useful. I mean, who has any need for a hunchback who stammers? That's how I wound up with Thaddeus. Sometimes he treats me like shit, I admit that—but he treats everyone else the same way. I'm happy here, because I've finally found a place where I can make a contribution and stop feeling like a parasite—"

"Are you calling me a parasite?" she interrupted.

"No, of course not," he answered her. "But after a lifetime of being ignored or pitied or merely tolerated, which is the worst of all, I finally feel like I'm earning my keep, and it feels good."

"I'm *trying* to earn my keep!"

"But until you figure out a way, why not at least do *something* and work the games?"

"Because then I'd just be Gloria Stunkel again."

"I don't understand," said the hunchback.

"Look at me, Tojo," she said, standing up and turning slowly around in front of him. "*Really* look at me. My face is plain, my eyes are too small, my nose is too big. I keep my body in good shape, but it's nothing to write home about: nobody from *Playboy* was ever going to put it in their centerspread. *This,*" she said, turning around again, "is Gloria Stunkel." She paused, staring sightlessly at an imaginary spot a few feet above Tojo's head, where a girl who was no longer Gloria Stunkel was strutting across a stage to a chorus of wild cheers and whistles. "But Butterfly Delight, she's something different. When I'm Butterfly Delight I'm not plain and clumsy and ordinary anymore. Butterfly Delight is beautiful and important. People actually pay money to watch her do nothing more than walk around a stage and take off her clothes. Men who wouldn't give Gloria Stunkel a second glance on the street howl like dogs when Butterfly Delight bumps and grinds; women envy her looks and her glamour. Butterfly Delight is someone *special*—and Thaddeus wants to kill her and make me go back to being Gloria Stunkel. Well, I'm not going to do it!"

"I'm sure it's just until we can get to a humanoid world," said Tojo soothingly.

"Humanoid?" she repeated sarcastically. "You mean like Mr. Ahasuerus—seven-foot-tall bald blue skeletons who look like they ought to be breathing fire? You think *they're* going to pay to watch Butterfly Delight?"

Tojo made no answer.

"It's just not fair," continued Gloria. "I don't just *like* my work, Tojo: I'm *good* at it." She opened a trunk that was next to her bed, pulled out a large vinyl-covered scrapbook with the Woolworth's pricetag still on the cover, and carried it over to him.

"Look at that," she said, opening it and pointing to an ad from a Wisconsin newspaper. " 'Back By Popular Demand,' " she read. " 'Butterfly Delight.' That's *me*, Tojo!" She continued thumbing through the pages, pointing out ads that

36

ran her photo, ads that mentioned she was the headliner, ads that implied she was Blaze Starr and Tempest Storm and Lili St. Cyr all rolled into one.

Tojo looked at the book and made properly impressed noises. It didn't matter that most of the ads were from theaters long since gone out of business, or currently running hardcore movies instead of burlesque, or piping in music as the girls danced for fifty businessmen on their lunch hours. It didn't matter that only two ads in the whole book were more than one column wide or an inch deep. It didn't even matter that none of them appeared in the journals of any city boasting as many as two hundred thousand people. In her chosen field Butterfly Delight was indeed a star, and it was hardly her fault that the bottom had fallen out of the field years before she had entered it.

"Who's this?" asked Tojo, coming to an eight-by-ten glossy photo of a tall, leggy brunette. "It looks very old."

"That's Gypsy Rose Lee," replied Gloria proudly. "She autographed it for me just before she died."

"That was very nice of her," said the hunchback.

"She was a very classy lady," responded Gloria. "Did you know that she played to more women than men during her career?"

"No, I didn't."

"It's true. Stripping doesn't have to be cheap and vulgar. It can be anything the audience will let it be. Ann Corio has been touring the country for the past fifteen years with an old-time burlesque show. Most of her audiences are families." She closed the book and tenderly returned it to the trunk. "I never saw a family audience in my life," she said at last. "All I ever got were freaks and drunks."

"You came along too late," said Tojo sympathetically.

"But I played as if my audience had class. I was always a *lady* on stage."

"I'm sure you were."

"I never let a customer touch me, and I never balled anyone to get work."

"Thaddeus used to complain about that all the time," said Tojo with a smile.

"After I'd been on the circuit for a few years, I found out

37

there was a school for strippers out in California, and I enrolled there to see if I could make my act even better. That's where Thaddeus found me."

"I remember. You were the best we ever had, Gloria."

"That's because I work harder at it than anyone you ever had. I jog two miles every morning. One hundred sit-ups. Stretching exercises. Constant dieting. I dance to my tapes every day. I never get out of condition."

"I know."

"This is what I am, Tojo. This is *me*. I can't help what my audiences were back on Earth, and I can't help not having them now. Gloria's just an ordinary girl who passes time between Butterfly Delight's performances. If I could be Butterfly Delight twenty-four hours a day, I would. I can't be, so I've made my adjustment—but I can't stop being her altogether. I just *can't!*"

Tojo stared at her long and hard, wondering what he could say and wishing he knew how to recognize the preliminary symptoms of a mental breakdown. He even found himself half believing in Butterfly Delight as a separate entity—not as a headlining stripper, but as the person who kept Gloria Stunkel sane for twenty hours a day. Suddenly he wished they had taken a doctor along, instead of the extra games barker.

Gloria had returned to her chair and seemed content to sit there, sipping her fruit juice and staring at the sequined gown that was still hanging on the closet door, but Tojo felt he had to say something, *anything,* to break the silence. His brain raced through hundreds of prior conversations he had had with her over the years, scanning them, trying to find some interest they had in common, or even some subject other than her work that she had ever shown any enthusiasm for. He was startled to discover that he couldn't come up with a single one, and wondered what to do next.

Finally she asked him if he would like a refill, and the sound of her voice breaking the grim silence of the room so startled him that he almost knocked his glass over.

"Yes, please," he said, not wanting one at all but suddenly afraid to offer her any rejection, no matter how trivial.

He was taken off the hook a moment later when Mr. Ahasuerus knocked on the door and entered the compartment.

"Ah, hello, Tojo," said the tall, cadaverous blue man. "I hope I'm not interrupting."

"No!" said Tojo, so anxious to force the word out that he almost screamed it.

Mr. Ahasuerus stared at him curiously, then turned to Gloria. "I'd like to speak to you for a moment, if I may."

"I'm not working the booths!" she said defiantly.

"This has nothing to do with the carnival," said the blue man.

"Oh?" she said, eyeing him suspiciously.

"Well, only insofar as everything that takes place aboard ship pertains, directly or indirectly, to the carnival."

"Will you get to the point?"

"Certainly," said Mr. Ahasuerus. "It has to do with something you requested from the galley robots. I believe you called it pineapple-papaya juice."

"What's the matter with that?" she said. "It's perfectly healthy. You might even try some yourself."

"The problem," he continued patiently, "is that our computer has nothing in its memory banks concerning the chemical composition of a papaya—so if it isn't absolutely essential to your health and well-being, would a substitute be acceptable?"

"I suppose so," she shrugged. "Make it banana-mango instead."

Tojo made a face at the thought of that concoction, and Mr. Ahasuerus shuffled his feet uncomfortably.

"I'm afraid there's something else as well," he said.

"Now it comes," she said, glaring at him.

"This bicycle you ordered. We're going to have to reprogram one of the robots, which will run into quite a bit of money, and I was wondering if it was really necessary."

"*I* think it is."

"But what is the purpose of a bicycle that doesn't *go* anywhere?" asked the blue man.

"It's an exercise machine," she said. "It keeps my legs in shape."

"Isn't there some less complicated way of so doing?" persisted Mr. Ahasuerus. "Running, for example?"

"Different muscles," she replied.

"And it is absolutely essential that you have this?"

She shrugged. "No, it's not absolutely essential."

"Then," he continued, "if it will not constitute too great a hardship . . ."

"Fine," she interrupted him.

"Thank you," said Mr. Ahasuerus.

"I'm doing you two favors," said Gloria. "I'm giving up my exercise machine and my papaya juice. Now I wonder if you can do me one."

"If it is within my power," said the blue man.

"You're an equal partner with Thaddeus," she said. "Why can't you book us onto some world where stripteasers are appreciated?"

"There *are* no such worlds," he said gently.

"I knew that son of a bitch lied to me!"

"No," said the blue man. "Mr. Flint knew that there were no worlds—except your own, of course—where stripteasing *existed*. He had no way of knowing that there were no worlds where it would be *appreciated*."

"But *you* did!" she snapped at him. "You could have told me!"

He shook his head. "You must believe me: I felt as Mr. Flint felt, that it would be a novel attraction that would delight audiences."

"Why would you think a bunch of lizards and birdmen would be interested?"

"Tunnel vision," he said with a shrug. "I have been a wanderer among the stars for so many years that I had forgotten how truly parochial local attitudes can be. I felt the fact that *I* found your act diverting meant that *everyone* would. I was mistaken, and I am sorry about it. But don't blame Mr. Flint. He is even more disappointed with the results of our tour, thus far, than you are."

"I find it very difficult to work up much compassion for Thaddeus," replied Gloria. "He's still bilking the marks and running the show and bedding every girl who works for him except me. He's making out just fine."

"He probably would be happy to debate the issue with you," said Mr. Ahasuerus.

"Once you sobered him up and pulled Jenny and Lori out of his bed, that is," said Gloria sardonically. "Look, Mr. Ahasuerus, I feel cheated and unhappy, and the last thing I need to hear from you is what a tough time poor old Thaddeus is having, okay?"

The blue man sighed deeply. "I don't know what you want me to say, Gloria. I truly had no idea so many of you were unhappy."

"What do you mean, so *many* of us?"

"Jupiter Monk thinks his lion is dying, Max Bloom wants to work at a game that will almost certainly kill him, Thaddeus is displeased with our choice of worlds. Everyone seems unhappy about something or other—except Billybuck Dancer, that is."

"The Dancer always *was* different," she said. "Let him shoot at things and spend his life dreaming that he's gunning down Doc Holliday and he's content. What does all this have to do with *me?*"

"I just thought you'd like to know you're not alone," said Mr. Ahasuerus.

"I'm more alone than I've ever been in my life," she replied unhappily.

"May I ask a personal question?" said the blue man.

"Why not?"

"I know why some of the others came with us—but why did *you?* You were a star on Earth."

"I thought I'd be a star out here, too," said Gloria. "At least, Thaddeus told me I'd be. And *you,*" she added, her eyes flashing, "never said different."

"And that's the only reason?" he asked. "To be a bigger star than you already were?"

"What's wrong with that?" she said defensively. Then she sighed. "No, it wasn't the only reason. All my life I've played in front of slobs. You saw the audiences at the meat show, Mr. Ahasuerus. They never even looked at me until I'd gotten out of my clothes. Just once, I wanted to perform in front of someone who appreciated what I was doing. Did you ever hear of Gypsy Rose Lee?"

The blue man shook his head.

"I was just talking about her with Tojo. She was the

greatest stripper that ever was. She used to talk to the audience about the stock market, and what books she'd read, and who made her gowns. They were so interested in that they didn't even care how much clothing she took off." She turned to Tojo. "She never had to worry about being Louise Hovack again. She was Gypsy. They even made a musical about her life."

"I know," said Tojo softly.

"And you think you'd like to talk about stocks and books to your audiences?" asked Mr. Ahasuerus, puzzled.

"Of course not!" she said. "My God, you're dense! I'm just using that as an example. She had a class act, and she played for class audiences in class theaters. They appreciated her art. They'd have been shocked if she rolled around on the stage and let them paw her, the way the carny strippers have to do. That's why I came: to find people who cared about how hard I was working instead of how easy I was."

"But if you have such contempt for you audiences back on Earth, surely you must be happier not stripping at all rather than stripping before them," said Mr. Ahasuerus.

"You don't understand at all!" she snapped. "I was a star on Earth. I was Butterfly Delight!"

"But if the audiences—"

"I didn't always work for the carnival," she said defensively.

"I see."

"Thaddeus misrepresented it to me," she added sullenly.

"Then why didn't you leave?"

"For what?" she snapped. "You think a bunch of drunken businessmen playing with themselves beneath folded newspapers are any better? They were *all* freaks and slobs!"

"I seem to have missed something," said the blue man. "If all your audiences were like that, then what benefit accrued to achieving stardom in such a field?"

"Because it made me better than them!" she yelled at him. Suddenly she began crying. "Dammit, it was the *only* thing that made me better!"

Mr. Ahasuerus turned to Tojo, a distressed expression on his gaunt face.

"What did I say?" he asked, thoroughly confused.

"It's all right," said the hunchback, getting off his chair

and walking over to put an arm around Gloria. "I think you'd better leave now."

"But . . ."

"She'll be all right," said Tojo, stroking her hair tenderly.

The blue man shook his head, sighed again, and walked out the door.

"I'm sorry," said Gloria, tears still trickling down her face. "I didn't mean to make a scene."

"It's all right," crooned Tojo. "It's all right."

"Do you have a Kleenex?"

He pulled a handkerchief out of his pocket and handed it to her.

"Thank you," she said, taking it and dabbing at her face. She looked up at him. "Did you know that when I was twelve years old I was the fattest, ugliest girl in my class?"

He whispered meaningless sounds and continued stroking her hair.

"It's true. I was such a homely little girl, I used to stare at myself in the mirror and wonder why God was mad at me. Even after I thinned down in high school, I was too awkward to make the cheerleading squad. I never even had a boy ask me for a date until my junior year. You should have seen him, Tojo," she said, a bittersweet smile on her lips. "He even made *you* look handsome and dashing."

"He sounds like my kind of person," replied Tojo, returning her smile. "Did he stammer, too?"

She shook her head. "I was so *average*, Tojo. Even after I stopped being fat I was just an average girl with average parents and average grades and average friends. I was always afraid I was going to have an average husband and sleep with him 3.4 times a week and have 2.2 children."

"But you didn't."

"Maybe I should have. That was the best Gloria Stunkel could hope for. If she didn't do that, she'd have been a waitress at some truckstop, or maybe a hooker. Not a call girl in a fancy apartment, but just some girl standing out there on a corner."

She had stemmed the flow of tears, but now they poured forth again.

43

"Maybe you'd better go," she said, wiping her eyes once more.

"If you're sure you'll be okay," he said doubtfully.

"Make him leave me alone and I'll be all right," she said. Tojo walked to the door.

"Promise you'll talk to him."

"I promise."

"Don't let him kill Butterfly Delight. I can't go back to being Gloria again. I just can't!"

He closed the door behind him, feeling for the first time in many years that there were worse things to be than an undersized hunchback with a speech defect, and wondering exactly who was cracking up: Gloria Stunkel or Butterfly Delight.

6.

"What are you talking about—cracking up?" demanded Flint.

He was sitting in Mr. Ahasuerus' office with his partner and Tojo, surrounded by the keepsakes of the blue man's thirty-odd years abroad in the galaxy. There were prints of sights he hoped he'd never see this side of delirium tremens, holograms of beings that he thought existed only in his nightmares, books in languages that no human would ever be able to decipher, plagues and knickknacks and curios of every imaginable variety and a few he didn't think *anyone* could have imagined.

The blue man's refrigerator—there was one in every room on the ship, but this was the largest outside of the kitchen— was filled with brown drinks and purple meats and oddly shaped canisters containing items that Flint didn't even want to think about, as well as a few cans of robot-brewed beer that were there strictly for his benefit and that tasted about the way he thought the brown stuff must taste. Still, he accepted a can, just to be polite, and was quietly furious with Tojo for claiming to be a teetotaler and not being forced to suffer equally with him.

Tojo sat on a couch of unearthly design—*all* of the blue man's furniture was unearthly, but this was a little more so than most—while Mr. Ahasuerus himself sat at his desk, sipping a cup of coffee, a beverage to which he'd become passionately addicted during his brief stay on Earth.

"Just what I said," answered Tojo. "Call it an identity crisis, or whatever you want, but she's getting awfully close to going off the deep end."

"It's true, Mr. Flint," interjected Mr. Ahasuerus. "I was there. I will support what Tojo says."

"Nothing personal, Mr. Ahasuerus," replied Flint, "but what the hell do *you* know about it? You entire experience has been with a carny crew. The next normal human you meet will be the first."

"Then let me say that I find her attitude abnormal even for a carnival worker," said Mr. Ahasuerus patiently. "I am concerned about her mental health and well-being, just as I am about all my employees."

"And besides, you wouldn't want her setting fire to the ship," added Flint sardonically.

"The ship is inflammable," the blue man pointed out mildly.

"This isn't a joking matter, Thaddeus," said Tojo.

"And you think letting her strip to an empty tent is going to make everything better?" Flint shot back.

"Of course not," said Tojo. "But I think you'd better realize that you've got a problem on your hands and start considering what to do about it."

"I've got more problems on my hands than I know what to do with," said Flint wearily. "You know I had to put a lock on the Bozo cage to keep old Stogie out of it?" He paused to light a cigarette. "Monk's lion is dying. Jenny and Lori are mad because I gave the Skillo game to Barbara. The Dancer tells me he's going to run out of bullets sometime next week. My partner tells me the Corporation is still sending their efficiency expert, even though we made thirty thousand credits our first three days here. Diggs got one of the Procyonians so hot that he took a swing at him last night and we damned near had a riot on our hands, the strip show couldn't draw flies at a watermelon party, this beer tastes like shit, and you think I've got nothing to do except worry about the fact that Gloria's unhappy?"

He leaned back in his chair, momentarily exhausted from

46

the recitation of his primary annoyances and wondering if he should even bother listing his secondary ones.

"It's not that Gloria is unhappy," said Mr. Ahasuerus, after waiting politely to see if his partner was through speaking for the moment. "We are all unhappy for one reason or another."

"Even you?" said Flint.

"Even me," said the blue man, exposing his teeth in his equivalent of a smile. "Seven months ago, I was a very successful tour guide."

"On the other hand, six months ago you were a very unhappy and unwilling freak show attraction," said Flint, returning his smile. "So things could be worse."

"Getting back to the subject at hand, the fact that Gloria is unhappy is not a major problem. The fact that she is having serious psychological and emotional disturbances could well be."

"Isn't it enough that I have to run this goddamned show?" said Flint. "Do I have to play nursemaid too?"

"I realize that empathy was never your strong point, Mr. Flint," said the blue man dryly. "Nevertheless, you should realize that it is in your best interest to do everything within your power to alleviate Gloria's problems."

"What do you suggest that I do?" asked Flint. "Send for forty sex maniacs from Hoboken?"

"I am sure you can think of something," said Mr. Ahasuerus. "As you yourself pointed out a few moments ago, I am hardly experienced enough to suggest a solution."

"Or take the responsibility for it," said Flint irritably.

"That's not fair, Thaddeus," said Tojo.

"What's *fair* got to do with anything, you ugly little dwarf?" demanded Flint. "We've got a girl both of you seem to think is cracking up, and you've just nominated me to play the part of her shrink. If you're worried about *fair*, maybe you ought to start thinking about whether putting her in my hands is fair to Gloria."

"Have you any alternative?" asked the blue man.

"Why not leave her alone and let her work things out on her own?"

"Because her problem, as Tojo has explained it, has been

47

caused by external forces with which she is incapable of dealing," said Mr. Ahasuerus.

"Well, short of my slipping each of the Procyonians a couple of credits to pinch her ass, I'm going to have just as much trouble dealing with it as she has."

They both stared at him in silence, and he began twitching uncomfortably.

"All right!" he snapped at last. "I'll think of something!" He glared at his partner. "Are you satisfied now?"

"Yes."

"Then you don't mind if I get the hell out of here?" said Flint, rising and walking to the door.

"Of course not. There is one last thing I'd like to say, though."

"Yeah?" said Flint, pausing in the doorway.

"I am sorry that my beer tastes like excrement," said the blue man, showing his teeth again.

"Don't let it worry you," said Flint. "It's not half as bad as your sense of humor."

He and Tojo left the office and took the elevator back down to the main level of the ship.

"I still don't know what he expects me to do," muttered Flint. "I mean, who the hell ever heard of a stripper with an identity crisis?" He shrugged. "Oh, well, I suppose we could be freezing in New Hampshire. Tojo, be a good little bastard and hunt me up some cigarettes."

"Where will you be?" asked Tojo.

"Around. I've got to check on Monk's lion, and do a couple of other things." He grinned ironically. "I'll be easy to recognize. Just look for a guy who keeps trying to convince himself he'd really rather be on this dirtball than Earth."

Flint turned and walked out the airlock, and a few minutes later was standing beside Jupiter Monk, looking at the listless lion that lay motionless in its cage.

"It's all these goddamned worlds," said the burly animal trainer. "He just can't make the adjustments."

"How old is he?" asked Flint, reaching his hand between the bars and stroking Simba's left ear. The lion paid no attention to him.

"Nine or ten."

48

"How old do lions get to be?"

"Older than this one," said Monk. "It's not age, Thaddeus. It's all these changes in his routine."

"Maybe we should have left him behind."

"What the hell was I supposed to do?" demanded Monk bitterly. "Turn him loose in the Vermont countryside?" He looked down at Simba. "He was born in a circus and he'll die in a carnival. I suppose that's fitting."

"How are the others doing?" asked Flint.

"Bruno's okay, and nothing seems to bother the leopards. But Jesus, I'm gonna miss this goddamned lion. He was the only one I could ever turn my back on. That fucking bear would sooner take my head off than look at me."

"Is there anything we can do?"

"For Simba? Not a chance. He's turned down his food two days in a row. A lion starts turning down meat, he's getting ready to die."

"Maybe we could spice it up with something," suggested Flint. "I could get the galley robots to make—"

"He's dying, Thaddeus!" snapped Monk. "It's not your fault and it's not mine, and it sure as hell ain't his, but pouring a little gravy over his food pan ain't going to put him back on his feet." Monk looked down at Simba again. "Best goddamned lion I ever had."

"I'm sorry," said Flint softly.

"It's all right. Nothing you can do about it."

"How much longer are you going to let him live?" asked Flint.

Monk shrugged. "When the time comes, I'll borrow a gun from the Dancer and take care of things myself. Another day or two, I suppose."

"I could see if Mr. Ahasuerus can program a robot to do it."

"It's my job," said Monk firmly. "I saw him into this world, I'll see him out of it."

"I always thought you captured him."

Monk shook his head. "Do you know how hard it's been to get any kind of animal out of Africa since they threw the British out? No, I had his mother in my old circus act." He reached his hand into Simba's mouth and rubbed his pale gums. "I've had him since he was born."

Flint couldn't think of anything else to say, so he stood quietly and watched Monk stroke the dying lion.

Finally the animal trainer looked up at him. "I've been thinking, Thaddeus."

"Yeah?"

"We're never going back to Earth, are we?"

"I doubt it."

"What the hell am I going to do when the other three die?"

Flint sighed. "Why don't we worry about that problem when we come to it?"

"You're the boss—but it's going to happen one of these days."

Flint spent another couple of minutes watching the lion tamer and the lion, then started walking back to the Midway. *Wonderful*, he thought grimly. *As soon as I figure out what to do with a stripper who hasn't got an audience, I'm going to have to deal with an animal trainer who hasn't got any animals.*

Maine and Vermont started looking better and better to him. Then Lori sought him out and tongue-lashed him for spending the past three nights with Jenny, and even his horrible two-week playdate on the outskirts of the Everglades on the Florida circuit seemed idyllic in retrospect.

As he was passing along the Midway on his way back to the ship, he saw Stogie and Diggs standing next to the Bozo cage, engaged in animated conversation.

"Damn it, Stogie!" he yelled, walking over to them. "How the hell many times have I got to tell you to keep away from the cage?"

"Relax, Thaddeus," said Diggs. "We're just entering into a friendly little wager."

"Yeah?" demanded Flint. "What kind?"

"My friend Max, here, has just bet me fifty dollars that I can't open this lock in less than five minutes." He gestured to the padlock on the gate to the cage.

"What do you know about picking locks?"

"Nothing," admitted Diggs. "But I know a hell of a lot

about betting. I figure any man who can manipulate a deck of cards as well as I can ought to be able to totally disassemble this thing with a tie pin in under three minutes."

"The bet's off," said Flint.

"Who the hell are you to tell me what I can and can't bet on?" demanded Diggs. "Or have you got something better to spend fifty American dollars on in this hellhole?"

"Just who do you suppose put the goddamned lock on in the first place?" snapped Flint.

"You?" asked Diggs, surprised.

"You bet your ass it was me."

"But I thought it was just to keep the natives out," said Diggs.

"It was to keep *him* out!" snapped Flint, jerking a thumb in Stogie's direction.

"Is that true, Max?" said Diggs reproachfully.

"He's got no right to stop me from being a Bozo if I want to!" said Stogie defiantly.

"Well, I'll be damned!" laughed Diggs. "You tried to flim-flam the old Rigger! What the hell do you want to practice for, Max? You'd probably drown in the first five minutes."

"Beats the hell out of dying of boredom," said Stogie sullenly. "You've seen Monk's lion, Thaddeus? That's *me* in two more weeks. Maybe nobody up here appreciates a good dirty joke, but at least let me go out as a clown."

"When did you ever tell a *good* dirty joke?" said Flint. "I'm running a goddamned carnival, not presiding over some kind of suicide ceremony. You want to feel useful, start spelling the Rigger at the Psychic booth."

"I'm an entertainer, not a con man!" snapped the old comic.

"Where have I heard *that* before?" muttered Flint grimly. He stepped over and stood next to Stogie, lowering his head until their faces were no more than three inches apart. "Now you listen to me, you senile prima donna! Monk's going to have an empty cage in another two days' time. If I catch you around *this* one again, I'm going to lock you in *that* one until you get all this *kamikaze* shit out of your system. Understand?"

"You don't have to yell at me," said Stogie, lowering his eyes and stepping back.

"The hell I don't! *Someone's* got to yell at a seventy-one-year-old man who wants to work the Bozo cage. Hell, do you even know how to swim?"

"Of course I do!" said Stogie defensively.

"You sure can't prove it by me. Why don't you practice in a bathtub every once in a while?"

"I didn't come here to be insulted!" raged Stogie.

"No. You came here to sneak into the goddamned cage and kill yourself." Flint paused, trying to control his temper. "Look," he said more softly, "if you *have* to be a clown, why not get together with the Dancer and see if you can work out some kind of routine?"

"With him shooting bullets all around me?"

"You'll be safer with him than in the cage."

The old comic lowered his head in thought. "I dunno, Thaddeus . . ."

"Think about it," said Flint. "And keep the hell away from here or you and I are going to have a race to see who kills you first."

"I'm sorry, Thaddeus," replied Stogie earnestly. "And I *will* think about working with the Dancer. It's just that . . . oh, I dunno: sometimes you get a little crazy when you start feeling useless."

"I know," said Flint.

He stayed and talked with them for a few more minutes, then checked with the Dancer to make sure he had given the robots some bullets so they could start duplicating them. Finally, when he had run out of chores, he grimaced and headed back to the ship and went up to Gloria's compartment.

"Can I come in?" he asked, standing in the doorway.

"It's your ship," she said, never looking up from the outfit she was sewing at her vanity.

"Not exactly," he replied, walking over and easing himself onto her recliner chair. "But I have a feeling that Mr. Ahasuerus and I are expected to pay off the mortgage." He lit a cigarette and she turned to him.

"I wish you wouldn't smoke in here."

"Sorry," he said, looking around for an ashtray, and

52

finally grinding it out on his boot and putting it into his pocket.

"It's bad for your cilia," she said seriously.

He grinned. "That sounds like the kind of straight line you used to feed Stogie."

She shrugged. "All right—kill yourself. See if I care. Just don't do it in here."

"What are you working on?" he asked, trying to change the subject.

"A new idea," she said, holding up some red satin material. "It's a breakaway blouse."

"What's new about breakaway costumes?"

"See this tab?" she asked, gesturing to a small piece of material perhaps an inch square just under the armpit. "Do you think the Dancer could hit it with his knife at say, sixty feet?"

"You want him to strip you with knives?" asked Flint, interested in spite of himself.

"I haven't spoken to him yet. Do you think he'll be willing?"

"He could kill you."

"Butterfly Delight isn't afraid."

"Maybe not, but Thaddeus Flint is. Besides, I think I've just got him a partner."

She glared at him. "I'm not working the booths."

"I know you're not. I've got *you* a new partner, too."

"Oh? Who?" she asked suspiciously.

"The best goddamned barker in the galaxy and points north," he summoned in his finest carny cadence. "In brief: me."

"What's the catch?"

"No catch," he replied. "It just seems that Butterfly Delight has got some friends in very high places, and they convinced me to give her one more chance. And what the hell—as long as it's a make-it-or-break-it proposition, you might as well have the best talker in the business telling these hicks what they're seeing."

"You mean it, Thaddeus?" she asked, her face suddenly radiant with happiness.

"Of course I mean it. But you're going to have to work alone. I can't pull Barbara and Priscilla out of the booths."

"When do I start?"

"What's wrong with tonight?" he said.

"Thank Tojo for me."

"Let's wait and see what happens. If they all walk out again, I may strangle him for you."

"You're not half as mean as you pretend to be, Thaddeus," she said with a smile.

"We could lock your door and put that theory to the test," he suggested.

"I have to work tonight."

"So?"

"It's bad for the wind."

He chuckled, shook his head, and walked out.

7.

"So where the hell are my cigarettes?" demanded Flint.

"Gone," replied Tojo. "You smoked the last of them this morning."

"What are you talking about? I brought fifty cartons along."

"We've been on the road for more than five months," said Tojo, "and you've been under a lot of pressure."

Flint was sitting in the mess hall, four empty beer cans lined up on the table in front of him.

"Then have the robots make up a batch!" said Flint irritably.

"They can't," answered Tojo uncomfortably.

"Of course they can," said Flint. "Just give 'em a butt to analyze."

"I tried," said the hunchback. "They refused to synthesize any cigarettes."

"What?" exploded Flint. "How the hell hard can it be to make a goddamned cigarette? They never have any trouble making fruit juice for your friend Gloria!"

Tojo shifted his weight.

"I'm waiting for an answer, you goddamned dwarf!" bellowed Flint.

"Mr. Ahasuerus told them that smoking was unhealthy," said Tojo, trying to force the words out quickly and stammering even worse than usual as a result.

"He did *what?*"

Tojo tried to answer him, but no words came forth.

"We'll just see about this!" snapped Flint. He got to his feet and stormed over to the elevator. A moment later he emerged on the top level of the ship, and a few seconds after that he was pounding furiously on the blue man's door.

"Do come in, Mr. Flint," said Mr. Ahasuerus politely, pressing a button that caused the door to slide into the wall, and Flint stalked into the room.

"I have somebody I want you to meet," said Mr. Ahasuerus, gesturing to a small, rotund, red-skinned being sitting on one of the couches. The visitor was dressed in a bright metallic fabric that seemed to change colors even as Flint looked at him.

"Who the hell are you?" demanded Flint.

"My name is Kargennian," said the red-hued being, standing up and extending his hand. "I work for the Corporation."

"I'll get to *you* later," said Flint harshly, turning back to Mr. Ahasuerus. "What's all this shit about not letting the robots make up any cigarettes for me?"

"It's detrimental to your health, Mr. Flint," said Mr. Ahasuerus calmly.

"Not as deterimental as getting your head shoved up your ass, Mr. Ahasuerus!" snapped Flint. "Unless you want a demonstration, you'd better countermand that order, and fast!"

"That is hardly the way to behave in front of our guest, Mr. Flint," said Mr. Ahasuerus, showing no sign of emotion.

Flint turned to face Kargennian again. "You're the hotshot efficiency expert?"

Kargennian smiled and nodded his head slightly.

"You tell this blue skeleton to have some cigarettes in my hands before sunset or you're going to see just how inefficient this joint can be after I go on strike."

He walked out without another word.

"Your partner?" inquired Kargennian dryly.

"He's inclined to be a bit emotional," said Mr. Ahasuerus.

"A *bit*?" said Kargennian.

Mr. Ahasuerus spent the next few minutes trying alternately to excuse and explain Flint's behavior, while Flint himself returned to the mess hall and sought out Tojo.

"It wasn't my fault," said the hunchback, prepared to duck an anticipated blow.

"Shut up and listen to me," said Flint. "He's here."

"Who?"

"The Corporation man. He's up there talking with Mr. Ahasuerus right now. I think," he added wryly, "that I could have made a better first impression."

"You didn't hit him, did you, Thaddeus?" asked Tojo, who half expected an affirmative answer.

"No. I was just my usual lovable self." He paused, lost in thought. "He must have arrived in the last hour or so, while I was down here drinking."

"I didn't see him pass through."

"Which just goes to show that you're about as observant as the rest of these slobs," said Flint. "Well, as long as he thinks I'm a little unbalanced, maybe we can use it to our advantage. He's pretty pudgy, and he's had a long trip." He nodded his head decisively, as if in approval of his train of thought. "I want you to show him every inch of the carny, Tojo."

"When?"

"The second he walks out of my partner's office. Don't give him a chance to rest or relax. If you get tired, have the Rigger spell you. Wine him, dine him, flatter him—but keep him going. Then pass the word that we're opening two hours later than usual tonight."

"I assume there's some purpose to this?"

Flint nodded. "A fat guy like him, all this activity's got to tire him out."

"I don't see the connection."

"I'm going to wake him up very early tomorrow morning for our meeting. That ought to take some of the starch out of him. Oh—and try to get a little cotton candy into him, or maybe a hot dog. Something his system's not used to."

"If you say so," shrugged Tojo. "Are you sure you don't want someone else to show him around, though?"

"Why?"

"You know—the way I talk."

"He'll have to concentrate that much harder to understand

57

you," said Flint. He paused. "By the way, you were always a heavy reader. Did you bring any books with you?"

"Of course."

"You don't mind if I borrow a couple?"

"Help yourself."

"Thanks." Flint stared at him. *"Well?"*

"Well what, Thaddeus?"

"Aren't you supposed to be hanging around Mr. Ahasuerus' office waiting for this guy to come out?"

Tojo opened his mouth to say something, then thought better of it and shuffled off to the elevator. Flint went to the hunchback's room, picked out a couple of books, tucked them under his arm, then went to Billybuck Dancer's quarters and knocked on the door.

"Come on in," said the Dancer, and Flint entered.

The room reminded him a lot of the Dancer's trailer back on Earth. The walls were covered with old tintypes of Wyatt Earp and Ben Johnson and Bat Masterson and Johnny Ringo and scores of other Western lawmen and outlaws, with a framed black-and-white photograph of the Dancer's parents sitting on one bedtable, and a picture—Flint couldn't tell if it was a photo or a print—of a young woman in a gingham dress on the opposite table. There were no books, no tapes, no records in the room, nothing but a pair of very plain chairs— the Dancer had ripped his recliner out and requested a hard wooden chair in its place—and a bed that seemed never to be slept in. The covers were wrinkled, as if a body had occasionally lain down on them, but Flint's guess was that the next time the Dancer crawled under the blanket and sheet would be the first.

"What do you want, Thaddeus?" asked the Dancer in his pleasant Texas drawl.

"I need a little help," replied Flint.

"You've already borrowed all my liquor," said the Dancer gently.

"I need some information."

"Ain't nothing I can tell you, unless you want to know about shooting or knife-throwing."

"Let's talk about Indians," said Flint, walking over to one of the chairs and sitting down.

The Dancer shrugged. "Suits me."

"Ever see a war dance?"

"Dwight Eisenhower was President when I was born, Thaddeus," replied the Dancer with a smile. "You ain't heard of an awful lot of Indian uprisings since then, have you?" He took a knife out of his pocket and started flipping it into the air. "That all you wanted to ask?"

"I've got more."

"Shoot."

They spoke for another half hour. Then Flint returned to his own room, sat on his bed, propped himself up against the headboard, and started skimming through the books he had taken from Tojo's room. He toyed with making notes, but decided that he spoke better off the cuff, so when he finished them just before twilight he placed them back in the hunchback's meticulously ordered bookcase.

He stuck his head out the airlock, saw that Tojo was escorting Kargennian around the Midway, and nodded in approval. Then he called Gloria on the ship's intercom system and told her that she wouldn't be performing for another two hours.

"Will these be satisfactory?" said a voice behind him, and he turned to find Mr. Ahasuerus standing there, holding a huge container filled with cigarettes.

"Thank you," said Flint sardonically.

"The pleasure is mine," replied the blue man with dry irony.

"How's the hotshot doing?" asked Flint, taking the container from him.

"Tojo has been showing him the Midway for the past few hours," said Mr. Ahasuerus. "I understand that we won't be opening for another two hours."

"That's right."

"Is there any particular reason?"

"None that you have to concern yourself with," replied Flint. "I suppose Kargennian wants to have a long talk with the pair of us after he's had a look around?"

"That is correct."

"Six o'clock tomorrow morning."

The blue man flashed his teeth. "You've never gotten out

59

of bed before noon in all the time I've known you, Mr. Flint."

"Just giving my all for the company," said Flint with a smile.

"You hope, of course, to wear Kargennian down," observed Mr. Ahasuerus.

"The thought had crossed my mind."

"To what purpose?"

"I'm sure I'll think of something," replied Flint. "First things first, Mr. Ahasuerus. Tonight I've got a half-crazy stripper to worry about. If you don't mind, I'll put off thinking about Kargennian until tomorrow morning."

"Is there anything you'd like me to do?" asked the blue man. "Don't look at me so suspiciously, Mr. Flint. I *am* your partner, and both of our careers are at issue, so to speak."

"Keep the hotshot out of the strip tent for the first couple of shows," said Flint at last. "I'm going to have enough trouble worrying about the marks without having to keep an eye on him too." He paused. "And don't tell him what time we're meeting tomrrow morning. We'll let it come as one of life's little surprises."

"As you wish."

Flint pulled a cigarette out of the container and lit it.

"How does it taste?" inquired Mr. Ahasuerus politely.

"About the same as the beer."

"You could always try to wean yourself away from them."

Flint merely glared at him, and after a moment the blue man shrugged and walked away.

He spent the next two hours in the mess hall, trying unsuccessfully to get used to the taste of the cigarette and trying to get over the urge to wretch whenever he inhaled, then gave the signal to open the gates and let the marks in. He studied them with a practiced eye, estimated that tonight's crowd would top three thousand, and hoped that Kargennian didn't come from some planet where forty thousand was a small turnout.

Still, he couldn't worry about it now, and he hunted up Swede, told him to spell Tojo, and requested that the hunchback report to him.

"How's it going?" he asked when Tojo had finally joined him.

"He's not such a bad guy, Thaddeus," replied Tojo. "He seemed friendly enough. All he really wants us to do is turn a profit."

"Never mind that. Did you manage to shove a hot dog into one end or the other?"

Tojo shook his head. "He didn't want any."

Flint grimaced, then shrugged. Maybe a hungry alien would be even easier to deal with than a sick one, especially if he didn't have time to eat breakfast before the meeting began.

"He seemed especially interested in the games," added Tojo.

"Yeah?"

Tojo nodded. "He was fascinated when I explained how the Psychic booth worked, and he made me spend about half an hour telling him every detail of the Auction scam."

Flint filed that information away for future use, then turned his attention to the problems of the moment.

"I want you to stick with me for an hour or so, Tojo," he said.

"Any particular reason?"

"We're going to try a new approach to the art of the striptease," he replied. "And if it works, I want someone who knows how to do it so I'm not stuck here every goddamned night. So keep your ears open, okay?"

"All right, Thaddeus."

"Now why don't you pop backstage and see if Gloria's ready?"

Tojo returned a moment later to say that she was just putting the final touches on her makeup.

"Good," said Flint, picking up a translator and hooking it onto his tie. "Now, as long as you're still on salary, get yourself a translator and get the marks into the strip tent—but don't tell them what they're going to see."

"What *will* I tell them?"

"You're a bright little bastard; you'll think of something."

"But—"

"Jesus H. Christ! There's three thousand marks out there,

61

all with money to spend. *Somebody's* got to be curious. Just get up on a platform somewhere and start sending them in.''

"Who'll be taking the tickets?" asked Tojo suddenly.

"Who do you think? Close up shop when you've passed about a hundred of them through, and we'll see what's what.''

The hunchback began his patter, wondering what the hell he was supposed to be selling, but to his surprise Thaddeus had been right. The carnival had played Procyon for a few days without a strip show, and the thought of a new attraction brought one hundred natives into the tent far more rapidly than he had expected.

"Welcome to the Pageant of the Ages," said Flint, when Tojo had closed the door and joined him inside the tent. "*The Ahasuerus and Flint Traveling Carnival and Sideshow* takes great pride and delight in presenting Earth's foremost interpreter of dance, legend, and myth—*Butterfly Delight!*"

He turned the translator off for the last two words so that Gloria could recognize her cue. Suddenly the tape deck was switched on, the rhythmic beat of "Stairway to the Stars" was piped in, and Gloria strutted onto the stage.

"I realize that the music may sound discordant to your ears," said Flint, switching the translator back on, "but it is our holiest of melodies, so please bear with us. What you are about to see is the Dance of Supreme Supplication, performed so that the Lord of Rain and Thunder, the great Apollo himself, will end the famine of our parched and thirsty world.

"Notice how the participant makes offerings to the mighty Apollo: a piece of fur, a length of cloth, transparent membranes that she has carried on her legs for this very purpose.''

Flint paused as the audience sat spellbound, trying to comprehend the cultural import of what they were seeing.

"Through the posture and gestures of her body, Butterfly Delight is now trying to direct the Lord Apollo's attention to the very spot where the lifegiving rain is most needed. Note the shimmying and twitching of her flesh: each minuscule gesture, all carefully controlled, gives further instruction.''

Gloria began a body-wrenching series of bumps.

"As you can plainly see, Butterfly Delight is now casting out the devils from the symbolic body of her nation, ritually cleansing the arid soil for the arrival of the much-needed rain. In a moment she will stand motionless for an instant, the holy music will cease, and she will bow in gratitude to the Great Lord Apollo for heeding her supplication. At this point we would appreciate it if you, as the congregation, would pound your hands together—not enough to hurt yourselves, but sufficient to make a rather loud noise—for only thus may we gain Apollo's attention and let him know of our appreciation."

Gloria's routine came to an end just as Flint finished speaking, and the audience, not wishing to offend the cultural or religious beliefs of another race, applauded as they had been instructed to.

"Well?" grinned Flint.

"I'm flabbergasted," responded Tojo.

"We'll do four more shows tonight: a mating ritual, a reenactment of the Rape of Lucretia (for which much thanks), a physical-fitness program, and some Indian sign language. Then we'll start eliminating the ones that don't seem to draw enough enthusiasm—or maybe we'll leave 'em all in for a couple of days. Once word gets out, who knows? Maybe the same marks will come back to see a different ritual."

The next four shows went smoothly, and it was a reasonably satisfied Thaddeus Flint who returned to the mess hall well after two in the morning to have a couple of beers.

He was sitting there, relaxing and still trying to smoke one of the robots' cigarettes without feeling as if his chest was on fire, when Gloria stopped by, glowing with satisfaction.

"We did it, didn't we?" she said with a happy smile. "We're back in business again!"

"We sure are," said Flint, answering her smile with his own. "Tojo'll take over tomorrow, and things ought to be back on track."

"I don't know, Thaddeus," she said doubtfully.

"About what?"

"Tojo. He's sincere, but he's not *you*. I don't know what you said to those crowds, but they stayed long enough to watch. Did you hear the applause I got?"

"You deserved it," replied Flint. "And don't worry about Tojo. He might even improve on what I did. He's going through his library right now, doing research."

63

"How do you research burlie patter in a classical library?" she laughed.

"Who said anything about meat-show patter?" said Flint. "You've got to adapt to conditions. Right now he's probably figuring out how to do Leda and the Swan."

"I don't understand."

"You don't think these goddamned Procyonians give a damn about naked human females, do you? I gave 'em some cock-and-bull about a rain dance, and another one about an Indian maiden describing a buffalo hunt through sign language, and——"

"What are you saying?"

"Just that you've graduated from Stripper to Cultural Interpreter."

"But I *am* a stripper!"

"To *me*, you are. To them, you're whatever I tell them you are."

"Did you tell them to applaud, too?" she demanded.

"No," he said. "That was their idea."

"You're a goddamned liar!"

"What's got you so upset?" he asked her.

"Don't you see?" she said, tears of frustration starting to appear. "It wasn't *me* they paid to see. It was your goddamned fairy tales. It was *you* who entertained them, not me! They don't even know what I was doing up there!"

"What's the difference?" he asked, unable to understand her outburst. "Gloria, these creatures don't even wear clothes. We filled the tent for Butterfly Delight and no one walked out before the end of the show. What the hell else do you want?"

She brushed a couple of tears off her cheek and stared at him. "I've had religious groups try to shut me down," she said at last. "But no one ever made fun of my act before tonight."

"Who made fun of it? I just *used* it."

"You just don't understand what I'm saying, do you?"

"Truthfully? No."

"I'm through. I'm not working for you anymore."

"Where are you going to go?" he asked with a gentle smile.

"I'll think of something. Maybe Mr. Ahasuerus' visitor will take me with him."

"What do you think you'll find on *his* world?"

"I don't know. But somewhere, somehow, I'm going to find someone who appreciates who I am and what I do."

She got up from the table and walked rapidly to the elevator.

Flint remained at the table, trying unsuccessfully to comprehend what had gotten her so upset. He was still working on it a few minutes later when Mr. Ahasuerus approached him.

"I hate to disturb you, Mr. Flint," he said apologetically, "but we have a bit of a problem on our hands."

"You've talked to Gloria?"

"No, I haven't. Why?"

Flint shrugged. "You tell me yours, I'll tell you mine," he said ironically.

"I have just received a message from John Carp."

"Fast Johnny?" said Flint. "Has he lined us up a couple of new worlds yet?"

"In point of fact, he has just tendered his resignation."

"Shit! Did he give any reason?"

"No," replied the blue man.

"And he's still shaped like a big gray slug?"

"To the best of my knowledge. And what is your particular problem?"

Flint sighed. "Go to bed, Mr. Ahasuerus. It'll still be a problem tomorrow morning. We'll talk about it then."

"You're sure?"

Flint nodded.

"Goodnight, then," said Mr. Ahasuerus. "I will see you in my office in"—he checked his timepiece—"just under three hours."

Flint winced at the thought, and then nodded.

He decided that there was no sense in going to bed himself, not with the meeting just a couple of hours away, so he walked through the airlock and began strolling along the Midway, hoping the cool night air might invigorate him.

A moment later he heard a single gunshot from the area of Monk's cages.

"Perfect," he muttered. "Just perfect."

8.

Flint yawned and glanced across Mr. Ahasuerus' office at Kargennian, hoping that the round little alien was sleepier than he looked. It wasn't as if Kargennian had hair, or more than one piece of clothing, but somehow he looked *groomed*. He also looked bright-eyed and bushy-tailed, and Flint felt a certain amount of loathing surging up inside himself: *no one* should look that goddamned alert on four hours' sleep.

"Are we ready to proceed?" asked Mr. Ahasuerus, taking a sip from his ever-present cup of coffee—which, Flint noted bitterly, tasted a lot more like real coffee than his beer tasted like real beer. As for the cigarettes . . . well, he hadn't had one in hours, and he still felt an urge to cough every time he took a deep breath.

"I believe so," said Kargennian. "That is, if you are equally ready, Mr. Flint?"

"Right," said Flint, wondering if he wouldn't have been better off with a nap the night before.

"Well, not to put too fine a point on it, the Corporation has been quite disappointed in your receipts up until your playdates on Procyon III," began the troubleshooter.

"I can't honestly say that my heart bleeds for them," commented Flint.

"I shall choose to ignore that remark," said Kargennian, and Flint shrugged. "To continue, your first five playdates

66

were one unbroken disaster, and I am not convinced you have the capacity to recoup your losses based on six game booths and a—what do you call him?—a sharpshooter.''

"We have other attractions," Mr. Ahasuerus pointed out.

"On the contrary, you have *no* other attractions worthy of consideration," replied Kargennian. "Circuses and carnivals are my field of expertise, and I assure you that the games and this Billybuck Dancer constitute your only assets. You've got a comedian whose jokes were probably not very funny on Earth and are incomprehensible anywhere else. You've got a girl who, for reasons unknown to me, thinks that shedding her clothing to music constitutes a money-making attraction.''

"It made money last night," said Flint.

"An aberration. I was *there*, Mr. Flint. I heard you during the last two shows. You and I both know that *you* were the only reason the audience remained. This might be acceptable if you were a barker, but you're the owner and manager, and this is profligately wasteful of such managerial talents as you may possess.

"To continue: you have an animal trainer who is *too* good at his job."

"Could you explain that?" asked Mr. Ahasuerus.

"Those animals are so well trained and obedient that most of the excitement has disappeared from his act, if indeed it was ever there."

"Maybe we ought to introduce you to Bruno and see just how tame *you* find him," said Flint dryly.

"I am merely offering you my evaluation, Mr. Flint," said Kargennian. "You have someone called Swede on your payroll whose function totally eludes me."

"He's a combination gofer and roughie."

"Whatever *that* may be," said Kargennian dryly. "You have four young females working the games, but two of them show a total lack of enthusiasm. I was unable to ascertain the function or whereabouts of one John Edward Carp. That leaves your gamesman, Diggs. He's good at his job, but he and Billybuck Dancer can't support the entire show." He paused, then added nastily: "According to our latest reports, Mr. Romany is doing far better with your old carnival back on Earth than you are doing out here.''

"Mr. Romany took over a show with thirty employees, a decent reputation, established routes and playdates, and three hundred thousand dollars' worth of rides," said Flint. "Don't try to impress me with what Mr. Romany is doing. He hasn't got enough brains to come in out of the rain. When he stops taking advice from Alma and Queenie and some of the others we left behind, he'll be broke inside of six months' time."

"That is neither here nor there," said Kargennian. "What we are concerned with is *your* carnival, and it is my considered opinion that it is never going to make a sufficient profit."

"Are you threatening to shut us down?" asked Flint ominously.

"I never threaten, Mr. Flint," said Kargennian. "If I decide to shut you down, I'll *do* it, plain and simple. There is an alternative, however."

"And what is that?" asked Mr. Ahasuerus politely.

"As I said, the show is not a total loss. The sharpshooter is brilliant, and I have never seen anything like your Psychic and Skillo games in my life. And this Auction routine that the little one—what was his name? Ah, yes: Tojo—that Tojo explained to me sounds like a scintillating concept."

"Get to the point," said Flint.

"The point, Mr. Flint, is that while you haven't the capacity to produce the necessary receipts, you *do* have certain assets—your games and your marksman—that certainly can be put to use."

"In what way?"

"The Corporation runs a number of carnivals and circuses," explained Kargennian. "I feel reasonably sure that I could arrange to have one of them annex your operation. I hasten to point out that there would be work for everyone, including yourself and Mr. Ahasuerus, as well as such employees as you wished to take along. Of course, the deal would revolve about Billybuck Dancer and your games expertise." He paused thoughtfully. "Yes, I think I can guarantee that we could arrange to have one of the shows assimilate your carnival with no loss of work or income to anyone."

"That's very generous of you," said Flint.

"Well, you're part of the corporate family now, and we *do* try to protect our own."

"How comforting," said Flint dryly. "Did you have a particular show in mind?"

"As a matter of fact," answered Kargennian, "there is a circus currently playing on Canphor VII that could easily accommodate your show."

"You don't say?" inquired Flint with a smile.

"Yes. The more I think of it, the more certain I am that that's the place for you. What do you say, Mr. Flint? If you're agreeable, I think we can make all the necessary arrangements before I leave this evening."

Flint laughed aloud. "*I* say that this is going to be easier than I thought!" He turned to the blue man. "Did you spot it?"

"It was the offer, wasn't it?" asked Mr. Ahasuerus.

"Of course it was."

"Would someone please tell me what is going on here?" demanded Kargennian.

"Why don't you trot outside and take a look at all the signs we've got posted on the grounds?" replied Flint.

"I don't understand," said the efficiency expert.

"If you'll read them, you'll see that this is *The Ahasuerus and Flint Traveling Carnival and Sideshow*. That's who owns it, and that's who's going to keep on owning it." He lit up a cigarette and almost managed to ignore the searing pain as he inhaled. "Let's see how much you've learned, Mr. Ahasuerus."

"Well, of course, if he *really* thought we were going broke, it wouldn't make much sense to assimilate us into another show, would it?" asked the blue man thoughtfully.

"You bet your blue ass it wouldn't!" said Flint. "If he thought we were going down the tubes, he'd cut us loose and let the Corporation take its losses."

"But I still don't see the reason for—"

"Sure you do," Flint interrupted. "I wasn't sure until he offered to save our skins for us, but now I know. Use your brain, Mr. Ahasuerus! He saw the games; he knows they're moneymakers. He saw the Dancer; he knows he can damned near carry the whole show on his back. He wants them so bad he'll be a real charitable soul and take the rest of us, just so we won't starve to death. Add it all up and what do you get?"

The blue man lowered his head in thought for a long moment, then jerked it erect. "Of course! He owns a piece of the circus on Canphor VII!"

"I didn't come here to be insulted!" snapped Kergennian, growing even ruddier in his anger.

"I know exactly why you came here, hotshot," said Flint. "Your fucking circus doesn't have anything to match the Dancer, and you don't know the first goddamned thing about running a game, so you thought you'd kill two birds with one stone: shut us down to score brownie points with the Corporation by showing them how well you're protecting their interests, and make a couple of bucks on the side by having your circus take us over."

"Mr. Ahasuerus, surely you're not going to let this . . . this *barbarian* make these ungrounded accusations!" demanded Kargennian.

"He *is* my partner," the blue man pointed out mildly. "And it has been my experience that Mr. Flint has a certain expertise at identifying particular . . . ah . . . character traits, shall we say? I think you may safely conclude that he speaks for both of us."

"I could always check with the Corporation," offered Flint. "If it turns out I was wrong, I'll apologize and you can have the whole damned show—lock, stock, and barrel. Of course," he added, still grinning, "you'll have to stay here under house arrest until they're through piercing the corporate veil."

"So what if I *do* own a piece of the circus—and it's a tiny piece, I assure you! How does that change anything?" said Kargennian defensively. "You're too small to make the kind of money you need merely to pay for your travel expenses."

"I was just coming to that," replied Flint.

"There is simply no way you can make ends meet with a show this size," persisted the ruddy alien.

"I know," said Flint. "So here's what you're going to do: you're going to ship us fifteen people—men or aliens, I don't care which—to work our extra games, you're going to ship us some rides, and you're going to get off our backs for the next three years.''

"I'll do no such thing!"

"Of course you will," said Flint easily. "Or we're going to have a little talk with the Corporation and tell them exactly what you were going to do."

"What makes you think they'll care?" said Kargennian.

"Come on now, hotshot," said Flint with a laugh. "If they didn't give a damn, you wouldn't have tried to talk us into it. You'd have just out and out ordered us to join your show." He paused. "Are you ready to talk a little serious business, now that all the bullshitting is over?"

"There is a word for what you are trying to do!" growled Kargennian sullenly.

"The word is blackmail," said Flint. "And I'm not just *trying*, sonny boy—I'm *doing* it."

"I *told* you he had qualities," said Mr. Ahasuerus in an amused tone of voice.

"Why should I give you all the things you want with nothing in return?" demanded Kargennian. "I may have private interests of my own, but I don't throw the Corporation's money away for no reason."

"Nobody expects something for nothing, not even me," answered Flint. "So we're going to make a little trade. You're going to give us something we want, and we're going to give you something *you* want."

"And what do I want?" asked Kargennian suspiciously.

"Granting that the Dancer is out of the question, you want to take somebody back with you who can show you how to run the games."

"I do?"

Flint nodded.

"And who are you going to give me? Diggs?"

"Not a chance," replied Flint. "Diggs, to borrow from the vernacular, is the franchise."

"Then who?" persisted Kargennian.

"I've got an employee who has expressed some slight interest in seeing other worlds that those that are on our agenda. We'll trade you Gloria Stunkel."

"Which one is she?" asked the pudgy alien.

"The one who takes her clothes off."

"She knows how all the games operate?" said Kargennian dubiously.

"She will, by the time I turn her over to you. And you get an added advantage: she'll keep doing her dance for your show."

"Out of the question," said Kargennian. "It's the least viable attraction I've ever seen."

"That's the deal," said Flint. "If she goes, she dances. Take it or leave it."

"I have a feeling it would create more problems than it was worth," said Kargennian, after some consideration.

"I'll toss in Max Bloom."

"Which one is he?"

"The comic. He'd make a great barker."

"Mr. Flint," said Kargennian slowly, "I may be unethical, but I'm not stupid."

"No one ever said you were," put in Mr. Ahasuerus.

"Then you'll forgive me if I decline the honor of taking all your problem cases off your hands, no matter how beautifully gift-wrapped they may be."

"Mr. Flint," said the blue man, "I do believe we could make do without John Edward Carp if we were forced to."

"I don't know . . ." said Flint, lowering his head in thought. Finally he looked up. "All right, Kargennian: we'll sweeten the pot even further. You can have Fast Johnny Carp—but it's gonna cost a little extra. I want a new animal for Monk, to replace the lion he lost last night."

"Mr. Flint, I don't believe you heard a word I said," replied Kargennian with a smile. "It is obvious to me that you can make do without Carp; he is nowhere to be found. And I have no idea what a lion is."

"A big cat, twice as big as the ones you saw in the show last night," said Flint. "We toss in Carp, you toss in a replacement animal."

"You're offering me two unhappy employees and an absent one!" snapped Kargennian in frustration. "What kind of fool do you take me for?"

"We are, of course, open to counteroffers," said Mr. Ahasuerus pleasantly.

72

"Diggs and Dancer are untouchable?" queried Kargennian.

"Right," said Flint.

"How about Tojo?"

Flint shook his head. "He's my bodyguard," he grinned.

Kargennian sighed. "You're making this very difficult, Mr. Flint."

"You're looking at it all wrong, hotshot," said Flint. "Whoever you take, you know they're going to show you how to work the games—and whatever you send us, you know we're going to use it to make money. You're going to make a profit, we're going to make a profit, and the Corporation's going to make a profit. And, of course, if we can't make a deal, there's always an alternative."

"Oh? What?"

"I can blow the whistle on you, in which case we'll still make a profit, and the Corporation will still make a profit, but you, my friend, are going to be out in the cold."

Kargennian glared at him for a long moment, then sighed again. "All right. I'll take the one who worked the Skillo game—provided that I be allowed to spend the afternoon with Diggs learning about the other games."

"Barbara?" mused Flint. "Well, what the hell, we haven't any use for a stripper."

"But will she go?" asked the blue man.

"How long do you need her for?" asked Flint.

"Four months ought to suffice," said Kargennian, leaning forward and getting down to business.

"I suppose if we put her on triple-time . . ." said Flint. "Hell, she was serving two years for pushing dope when I sprung her back in Massachusetts." He nodded his head sharply, then looked at Kargennian. "Okay, let's get this thing straight. You're going to pick Diggs' mind this afternoon, and borrow Barbara for four months."

"Possibly six," interjected Kargennian.

"Four," said Flint firmly.

Kargennian shrugged and nodded his agreement.

"In exchange for this, you're going to have the Corporation send us fifteen games workers, and a pair of rides, and an animal for Monk."

"What type of rides?"

73

"Oh, I think a Ferris wheel and maybe a Tilt-a-whirl," said Flint.

"I've never heard of either of them."

"No, I don't suppose you would have. All right: you tell me what's available, and I'll choose."

"One Class A and one Class B," answered Kargennian.

"What's the difference?"

"Class B is for children."

"Deal," nodded Thaddeus. "And Monk needs an oxygen-breathing carnivore."

"It can be arranged," said Kargennian. "How long will you need the workers for?"

"They're staying."

"But you're only giving us Barbara for four months!"

"Yeah, but Barbara is *ours*. You're just giving us the Corporation's workers; nothing is coming out of *your* pocket."

Kargennian stared at him for a moment. "Done," he said finally.

"Good," said Flint. "Now, that wasn't so hard, was it?"

"I wonder why the Corporation ever made an accommodation with you in the first place," said Kargennian sullenly.

"For the same reason *you* made an accommodation."

"And what was that?"

"No choice," grinned Flint. He stood up and stretched. "And now, Mr. Ahasuerus, if you think you can handle the choice of our rides, I've got to go tell Barbara to pack." He walked to the door and stopped.

"Hey, Kargennian?"

"Yes?"

"Tell you what. You were such a good loser, I'll toss Gloria in for free."

"To work the games?"

"To strip."

"No, thank you, Mr. Flint."

"You're sure? You'd be making her very happy."

"Making people happy isn't my business, Mr. Flint," said Kargennian.

Flint shrugged, left the room, and tracked Barbara down in the mess hall. She didn't like the idea of being the only human in Kargennian's circus, but the thought of four months' triple-time pay weakened her resolve, and finally she consented, without—Flint thankfully noticed—ever once wondering where she would be able to spend her newfound riches.

Then he went up to Gloria's room, knocked on the door, and waited for her to open it.

"What do *you* want?" she said coldly, but stepped aside to let him in.

"I want to tell you that I tried my damnedest to get the efficiency expert to take you with him, and he turned me down cold."

"I'll just bet you tried!"

"I did. You can ask Mr. Ahasuerus."

"Then I'm stuck here," she said dully.

"For the time being," Flint replied. "However, now that I've introduced the notion of trading personnel around, I think it's just a matter of time before we can place you somewhere where you'll be happier."

"Who did you trade?" she asked, interested in spite of herself.

"Barbara."

"I'm ten times the stripper she is!"

"He didn't want a stripper. Barbara's going with him to show his crew how to run the games."

"I'll bet she convinces him to let her strip," said Gloria bitterly.

"No chance," said Flint. "First of all, she doesn't like stripping. And second, round little red things aren't going to want to watch a woman take off her clothes any more than the birdmen did."

"You really tried?" she asked at last, looking into his eyes.

"I really did."

"Then it's over," she said softly. "It's over, and Butterfly Delight is dead, and I'm here forever." She lowered her head for a moment, then said: "Damn you for ever meeting me, Thaddeus Flint." She took a deep breath. "Tell the Rigger I'll report for work tomorrow morning."

Flint walked out of the room, and Gloria Stunkel lay on her bed, and cried, and mourned the unheralded passing of Butterfly Delight, the greatest artiste and ecdysiast in the galaxy.

9.

"Okay now, love," said Diggs, lighting a thin cigar and pushing his straw boater back on his head, "let me show you how the shell game works."

"You just put a pea under one of the shells and move them all around," said Gloria, stepping closer to the booth's counter to keep out of the sun.

"Sounds pretty simple, right?" grinned Diggs.

He took a pea, placed it under one of the three shells, and began moving them slowly around the counter.

"Okay," he said after a moment. "Where's the pea?"

Gloria pointed to the left-hand shell, and Diggs picked it up, revealing the pea.

"Pretty good," he said, still smiling. He covered the pea, moved them around again, and then looked at her questioningly. "And now?"

She pointed to the middle shell, and again she was right.

"You're a very perceptive young lady, my dear," said Diggs. "Let's try it one more time—only this time, let's make it a little more interesting. Shall we bet a dollar?"

Gloria shrugged and nodded.

Diggs began moving the shells again, even slower than before. His hands, which could appear as little more than a blur when shuffling a deck of cards, seemed almost to be moving in slow motion. At last he was finished.

"Well?"

"The middle one," said Gloria.

Diggs picked up the middle shell, and pursed his lips in mock sympathy when no pea appeared.

"Too bad, my dear," he said, trying not to laugh. "But just because of my generous nature, I'm going to give you a chance to win your dollar back. I'll bet you five to one that you can't guess which shell the pea is under."

"Without moving them again?" she asked suspiciously.

He said nothing, but folded his arms behind his back.

"The left one," said Gloria.

"Pick it up," replied Diggs.

She did so. There was no pea.

"Damn!" she said. "I had the funniest feeling that it was on the right all along."

"Care to bet?" grinned Diggs.

She reached out and picked up the shell.

"Where did it go?" she demanded.

"Well, now," he chuckled, "that's what you're here to learn, isn't it?"

"You cheated!" she said accusingly.

" 'Cheat' is an ugly word, love," grinned the Rigger. He reached a hand out and pretended to pluck the pea from behind Gloria's right ear.

"You palmed it!"

"Actually, I didn't," he smiled. "This is a different pea. Keep your eye on the table."

He touched a small button with his foot, and a tiny hole appeared.

"All you have to do is remember where the hole is, so you know where to place the shell with the pea. This second pea is just to keep the suckers from wondering what happened to the first one." He paused. "Simple, but effective."

"Simple, but dishonest," said Gloria.

"You're being too harsh, my dear," he said. "After all, we played three games and you won two of them."

"No matter how you justify it, it's still dishonest," said Gloria.

"You mustn't rush to moral judgments of your peers,"

said Diggs. "After all, I don't complain about the fact that you disrobe in public."

"What I do is an *art*!"

"I will grant that for the sake of argument," said the Rigger. "But by the same token, you must accept that what we do at the game booths is also an art."

"What's artful about putting a hole in the counter?" said Gloria contemptuously.

"For that matter, what's artful about breakaway clothing?" replied Diggs calmly. "Both are devices designed to make our jobs a little easier. You would manage to remove your clothing even if you had to rely on buttons and zippers, and I would manage to fleece the marks even if I had to rely on nothing but my skill. But neither of us likes making things hard on ourselves, and so we use mechanical assistance whenever possible."

"It's not the same thing."

"Of course it is."

"I entertain people. You bilk them."

"Of course I bilk them," laughed the Rigger. "They come here to be bilked. And I give them their money's worth. I always lose the first game, no matter what game I'm playing. I tell jokes. I huff and puff, I strut, I roar like Monk's dear departed lion, I bluff and bluster, and I play the game like my life depended on it. They get their money's worth from the entertainment alone."

"You could entertain them without cheating them," said Gloria.

"Not really. I'd be concentrating too hard on winning. This way we all have a good time." Gloria just glared at him, and he took a deep breath and continued. "You object to the nature of my business. Well, love, I object to the nature of yours. I was working the carny circuits before they had anything stronger than a hootch dancer who'd get out there in half a ton of silks and robes and shimmy for five minutes. You say I don't show the marks everything I'm doing. Perhaps not. But you show them things that only your lover ought to be looking at. Which of us is the less moral?"

"I work at my craft," she said defensively. "I give them their money's worth. I don't try to rob anyone."

"You think I don't work at *mine*?" he responded. He reached into his pocket, pulled out a deck of cards, shuffled it vigorously for a few seconds, and dealt out four five-card hands. He turned them up in turn, revealing that each possessed a royal flush. "May I suggest that this takes even more skill than copulating with the curtains?"

"Don't you ever feel sorry for them after you've fleeced them?"

"Ever been to a slaughterhouse?" he replied. "Do you feel sorry for the hamburgers you eat?"

"Yes, I do!" she snapped. "That's why I became a vegetarian!"

"Gloria, the world—hell, the whole damned universe—is divided into just two groups: meat eaters and meat. It has been my experience that the former never feels sorry for the latter. As Thaddeus says, it might even be sacrilegious."

"Well, you and Thaddeus can do what you want, but I'm not going to cheat. It's immoral, and nothing you can say is going to change my mind about it."

Diggs sighed. "All right," he said at last. "Let's go up the row and see what the hell we can find for you to do."

"How's she working out?" asked Flint, as the crowds started departing an hour after midnight.

"Just awful," said Diggs, shaking his head sadly.

"In what way?"

"Thaddeus, for a girl who's worked the carny circuit for a couple of years, she just doesn't seem to know how things work around here."

"How the hell can she mess up the bottle booth?" demanded Flint. "She takes their money, gives them three throws to knock the bottles over, and that's the whole of it."

"I keep showing her how to set them up," complained the Rigger. "You know, putting them in the shadows, centering them on the bench, reaching over the counter to hand out the balls so the mark is a couple of feet farther away, and she just won't do it. And hell, she sets 'em up so unsteadily that you could practically blow 'em over."

"What's the bottom line?" sighed Flint.

"She took in nine hundred credits."

"Not bad."

"And she gave out twelve hundred credits' worth of prizes."

"So give her some slum."

"She won't display it," said Diggs. "She keeps pointing out the good stuff to the marks."

Flint shrugged. "We can take a three-hundred-credit-a-night beating until I figure out what to do with her."

"It's going to get worse," said the Rigger.

"Yeah?"

Diggs nodded. "The marks lose everywhere else and they win at her booth. It starts them thinking, if you know what I mean."

"I see your point," replied Flint with a grimace.

"Can't you let her go back to stripping?" persisted Diggs. "It's all she talks about anyway."

Flint shook his head. "Out of the question."

"But you filled the tent last night."

"It's a matter of aesthetics, not customers," said Flint wryly.

"I don't understand."

"Welcome to the club," said Flint.

Diggs returned to supervise the closing of the booths, and Flint wandered over to the mess hall. He dialed a cup of coffee and a sandwich, specifying that the meat could be anything except blue, and joined Tojo, who was sitting alone at one of the tables.

"How'd it go tonight?" he asked, pulling up a chair.

"We sold out all three shows," replied the hunchback. "The Dancer had to adjust and do a few extra tricks, since Monk's show is a little shorter without Simba, but it went over okay. He's fantastic!"

"Who?"

"The Dancer."

"You spent your whole life wanting to be a barker," smiled Flint. "Now that you're a barker, have you decided you'd rather be a trick-shot artist?"

Tojo shook his head. "I'm happy doing what I do. But I can admire him, can't I?"

"As long as you remember that he's a little crazy."

"We all are," replied Tojo with a smile.

"Him more than most," said Flint seriously.

"How did Gloria do?"

"Don't ask," said Flint.

"That badly?"

"Sometimes I think that in her own way she's as mad as Wyatt Earp. At any rate, she's a hell of a lot more self-destructive."

They fell silent for a few minutes while Flint ate his sandwich and finished his coffee. Then Mr. Ahasuerus walked through the airlock, spied them sitting together, and wandered over.

"Did the hotshot get off okay?" asked Flint idly.

"Two hours ago," replied the blue man. "What's this I hear about a magician?"

"A magician *or* a juggler," said Flint. "It's up to him."

"Why are we getting either?"

"Kargennian wants to run a three-card monte game, so I traded him one of the Rigger's marked decks for an entertainer. I figure the specialty show can use another act." He paused and allowed himself the luxury of a small grin. "And the deck only cost three dollars back on Earth."

"I feel very fortunate to have you as my partner, Mr. Flint," said the blue man.

"You should, Mr. Ahasuerus," replied Flint. Suddenly the smile vanished from his face. "Anything further from Fast Johnny?"

"Not a word."

"If he doesn't come back, who's on the hook for his ship—us or the Corporation?"

"I suspect that we are," replied Mr. Ahasuerus. "After all, he was a carnival employee on carnival business, and as best I can determine he is not being held against his will."

"How much is the ship worth?"

"More than we can possibly afford," answered the blue man.

"Shit!" snapped Flint. "Well, he's not going anywhere. We'll let it ride for a few days, until we work the new crew into shape. When are they due to arrive?"

81

"Two days from now."

"Good. Then we'll only be without the bottle booth for two nights."

"Gloria's not working out?" asked the blue man.

"She's not exactly dogging it," said Flint. "She's just not cut out to be a con artist." He shook his head. "Hell, I wonder if she was cut out to be anything but a stripper."

"What shall we do with her, then?" asked Mr. Ahasuerus.

"Who knows?"

"I have a suggestion," interjected Tojo.

"Yeah?"

"Well, she's more of an entertainer than a games operator, and Monk's act is running short with Simba dead. Maybe we can work her into it somehow."

"You know, that's not half bad," mused Flint. "A pretty girl sticking her head into a leopard's mouth, something like that. It might dress up the act."

"Will Monk agree to it?" asked the blue man.

"You make it sound as if he's got a choice," said Flint. He lowered his head in thought for a moment, then looked up again. "Yeah, that just might work out all the way around. Every now and then you come up with a decent idea, you ugly little dwarf."

"Thank you," said Tojo.

Flint rose from his chair.

"Hunt her up after she knocks off work for the night and tell her to get her ass over to the training cage tomorrow morning," he said as he left the mess hall.

"Tojo, do you mind if I ask you a question?" said Mr. Ahasuerus after Flint had departed.

"Not at all."

"Why do you let him speak to you like that?"

"You asked me that question back on Earth," Tojo said with a smile.

"I know. But if I'm to spend the next few years with Men, I really should make an effort to understand them, and I seem to be having some difficulty."

"He's rude to everyone."

"But he is especially abusive to you," said the blue man.

82

"He likes me better. It's his manner."

"You could ask him to moderate it."

"Why bother?" asked Tojo. "He's not going to change. I probably wouldn't recognize him if he did."

"But these remarks he makes about your appearance . . ."

"They're mostly true," said Tojo with no sign of self-consciousness. "I *am* ugly and I *am* little. Would it make you happier if he called me a hunchback instead of a dwarf?"

"No," said Mr. Ahasuerus, shaking his head in bewilderment. "If it doesn't bother you, I don't know why it should bother me. But as long as you don't seem to mind discussing your . . . ah . . . physique, I have another question. You've seen what our surgeons have been able to do to Fast Johnny, and what they did to Mr. Romany before he went to Earth . . . ." He paused and looked across the table at Tojo.

"And you want to know why I haven't asked them to straighten my back?" smiled Tojo.

"Well, yes," said the blue man uncomfortably.

"All my life I've tried to be accepted for what I am," said Tojo. "I've taken thirty years of abuse and teasing and ridicule and pity."

"All the more reason, I should think."

Tojo shook his head. "Now I'm doing what I want, and I'm doing it well. I pull my weight, I'm accepted as a useful member of the carnival, and I did it on my own terms. If I changed my shape now, it would make all the abuse and ridicule meaningless."

"I don't quite see it that way," said Mr. Ahasuerus.

"Then let me put it as simply as possible: I know that I'm happy right now, the way I am. I don't know for a fact that I'd be happy if I was like everybody else."

"But that's ridiculous."

"Maybe so," said Tojo with a shrug. "But I haven't been happy long enough to take the chance. Let me enjoy myself for a few months or a few years. Then maybe we'll talk about it."

"If that is your desire," said the blue man.

"It is. And don't start feeling sorry for me," said the hunchback seriously. "No one else does—including me."

83

The blue man watched him get up and shuffle out through the airlock in search of Gloria, and reflected upon how much he still had to learn about this odd race into whose company, for better or worse, Fate had thrust both him and his career.

"All right," said Monk. "I'm gonna keep his muzzle on until he gets used to you. Step through the door now."

He was standing in the center of his training cage, a structure of canvas flooring and titanium bars perhaps fifty feet in diameter. Gloria, dressed in jeans and a sweatshirt, stood at the barred door, staring apprehensively at Bruno the Bear, who despite his muzzle was not a particularly reassuring sight.

"You sure he won't hurt me?"

"He's just a big playful puppy," said Monk, ducking a swipe of Bruno's paw that would have decapitated him if it had landed.

"I didn't like the looks of that," said Gloria hesitantly.

Monk slammed the handle of his whip into the bear's belly. "Don't worry about it," he said, watching Bruno out of the corner of his eye. "If push comes to shove, he'd much rather kill me than you."

"Okay," she said, stepping gingerly into the cage. "But I'm staying by the door."

"Gloria, get out in the middle," said Monk. "For what it's worth, if he wants to get out of here, that door sure as hell ain't going to stop him."

Gloria took another step, then stopped as Bruno emitted a low, rumbling growl.

"I'm scared!" said Gloria.

"I won't let him hurt you," said Monk patiently. "Just walk out into the center of the cage."

"I can't."

"The hell you can't."

"Damm it, Jupiter—I'm about two seconds away from wetting my pants."

"Come on, Gloria—you've seen me wrestle with him when he's not wearing a muzzle. Let's get this show on the road."

She took another tentative step, froze as Bruno growled again, and then stepped back to the door.

"There's nothing to be afraid of as long as I'm here with him!" snapped Monk.

"Maybe not for you."

"What the hell's the difference?"

"Look, Jupiter. I'm scared. I'm sorry, but I'm scared to death. Maybe you'd be scared if you had to strip in front of six hundred screaming women. It just affects people differently, that's all."

"Well, if you won't work with him, you won't work with him," said Monk. He whacked Bruno on the shoulder with the flat of his hand. "Get over there!"

The bear snarled and lumbered to the far side of the cage.

"Now stay put!" snapped Monk. He backed away couple of steps, then walked over to Gloria.

"I suppose if you can work with the cats, I can still use you."

"I'll try," she said tightly.

"Okay. Back off while I get Smokey the Bear out of here."

He unsnapped Bruno's chain and collar from where they were hanging on the door, walked over, ducked another swipe of the bear's forepaw, attached the collar, and hooked the chain on.

"All fours!" he shouted, and the bear, which had been standing erect, lowered his front feet to the canvas. Monk led him out the door while Gloria backed off to give him plenty of room, took him to a nearby holding cage, and locked him in it.

Then he rolled the cage containing his two leopards—one spotted and one black—up to the door of the training cage, hit a catch, and released them into the larger cage.

They frisked around like kittens for a few minutes. Then Monk walked into the cage carrying a pair of stools, set them down at opposite sides, walked out, and returned once more with a large hoop.

He cracked his whip twice, and the leopards each jumped onto a stool.

"Okay," he said to Gloria, who was standing just outside the door again. "This is an easy one, but it looks pretty good to an audience. Stand about six feet away from this guy here," he said, positioning himself near the black leopard, "hold the hoop out like so, and holler: 'Jump!' "

As he said the word the black cat hurled himself through the hoop, hit the floor running, and circled the cage, winding up atop his stool again.

"Nothing to it," said Monk with a smile. "Of course, we'll set fire to the hoop for the performance."

"Won't that burn him?" asked Gloria.

"He goes through it too fast to feel the heat," explained Monk. "And of course it won't be burning at the point where you hold it. We let each cat do it once. Then we move the stools about twelve feet apart, and then they'll jump together and wind up on each other's stool. You'll have to hold stock-still for that one, though. There's not a hell of a lot of room when they're both passing through it, and if you move, one of 'em's going to get burned." He walked to the door. "Ready to take a shot at it?"

Gloria took a deep breath and nodded.

"Try not to look so red in the face, a nice pretty girl like you," smiled Monk. He led her into the cage and handed her the hoop.

"Don't I get a whip or a gun or anything?"

"Do you know how to handle a whip?" he asked.

"No," she admitted. "But I'd feel a lot safer with a pistol in my pocket."

"I've already killed a quarter of this act with a pistol," said Monk grimly. "That's enough shooting for the time being." He walked over to the bars and leaned against them. "Anytime you're ready."

Gloria walked slowly, carefully, to the center of the cage, then hesitantly approached the black leopard.

"Is this close enough?" she asked at last.

"Another couple of feet," said Monk.

"You're sure?" she said. "You looked like you were this far."

"Two more steps," Monk answered firmly.

Gloria took two very small steps.

"All right?" she asked, never taking her eyes off the leopard.

"Fine. Now hold up the hoop and holler 'Jump!' at him."

Gloria held the hoop out very stiffly. The leopard curled his lips back and growled.

"Just clearing his throat," said Monk easily.

"You're sure?"

"I'm sure. Just don't look so hesitant or you'll make him nervous."

"Him?" repeated Gloria. "What about *me*?"

"Just tell him to jump."

Gloria looked at the leopard again, held the hoop out rigidly, and said, "Jump!"

The black leopard leaped from his stool with a roar, and Gloria dropped the hoop as he was passing through it and ran toward the door. The cat got tangled in the hoop and fell to the canvas. He was up again in an instant, growling furiously. Suddenly he saw a flash of movement as Gloria reached the door and instinctively hurled himself after her.

Monk bellowed a curse and dove for the leopard, grabbing his tail just as his head was passing through the open door. The cat turned, hissing, and lashed out with a forepaw. Monk took the blow on his shoulder, cursed again, and struck the cat in the face. The leopard, startled, backed off, hissing and snarling, and now its companion leaped down from its stool and began slinking toward Monk. The trainer got to his knees, clutching his shoulder.

"Shut the fucking door!" he bellowed.

"You're bleeding!" cried Gloria, closing the door behind her.

"That's a lot less than you're going to be if I get my hands on you!"

"I'm sorry! I just panicked when I saw him jumping at me!"

The door began cracking open.

"Latch the goddamned thing!" hollered Monk.

Gloria fumbled with the catch for a minute before it fell into place.

"I'm sorry, Jupiter," she began.

"Shut up!" snapped Monk, swinging a blow at the leopards to remind them to keep their distance. "That's the first time I've been nailed in five goddamned years."

"I didn't mean to run," said Gloria, staring in horrified fascination as the blood began seeping through Monk's shirt.

"Just get the hell out of my sight, and send someone over here with some antiseptic and a roll of gauze—and don't you *ever* come near my animals again!"

She ran to the ship for medical help as Monk glowered at the black leopard.

"What the hell is left?" said Flint, popping open a can of beer and peering glumly out through a porthole.

"Maybe we *ought* to let the Dancer shoot her clothes off," offered Tojo.

"How did you know about that?"

"She mentioned it to me," said the hunchback. "Even if the audience doesn't know what stripping is, it might be a novel trick."

"And if she flinches like she did with the cat, have you got a graveyard picked out?" asked Flint. He took a long swallow. "You know, Stogie decided not to work up a routine with the Dancer, and he's a lot more interested in dying than she is." He paused, staring at his beer can. "Maybe we can kill two birds with one stone."

"What do you mean?"

"Stogie and Gloria."

"I don't follow you," said Tojo.

"Maybe they can work out a routine together."

"But no one understands Stogie's jokes," said Tojo. "They're all dirty, and these beings just don't relate to that."

"So we'll have them work out a slapstick routine," said Flint. "All pantomime."

"Can they do it?" asked the hunchback dubiously.

"Who knows? At least it can't be any worse than his working the Bozo cage and her playing with Monk's cats."

*   *   *

"Well," muttered Stogie just before he and Gloria walked out onto the makeshift stage in the specialty tent, "it ain't New York—but at least we're working."

They had spent a full day working out a skit, rehearsing their pratfalls, practicing their mugging. Then, before trying it out on the Procyonians, Flint had suggested a practice run in front of the human crew to determine whether they were at least funny by normal standards, and Stogie had agreed.

Now the moment was upon them, and the skit began. The old man was no longer Stogie the burlesque comedian; he was once again Max Bloom, the vaudeville headliner who could get laughs just by raising an eyebrow, who no longer needed to use four-letter words and obscene gestures to keep an audience's eyes from straying eagerly to the wings.

"You know," whispered Tojo excitedly to Flint, "he reminds me of Harpo Marx!"

"Better," replied Flint softly.

"Then why isn't anyone laughing?"

"Because he's not playing off of Chico or Groucho up there," said Flint, as Gloria missed a cue, took a pratfall before Stogie stuck out his leg to trip her, and anticipated too quickly a number of obscure items he withdrew from a seemingly bottomless pocket.

When it was over, everyone—Monk, the Dancer, Swede, Diggs, Flint, Tojo, and the girls—applauded politely, and all of them except Flint left the tent.

"Where's Gloria?" asked Flint as Stogie approached him.

"Cleaning up. She'll be by in a couple of minutes." Stogie paused and looked at him, his face flushed with excitement. "Well Thaddeus, are we in business?"

"*You* are," replied Flint. "I had no idea you were this good, Max."

"I felt sharp!" enthused Stogie. "I felt *alive* again! It's been a long time between dirty jokes, Thaddeus."

"Can you work up a single routine?" asked Flint. "Maybe an Emmett Kelly kind of thing? You know—go around the grounds entertaining the kids, leading them to the attractions, sort of like the carny's goodwill ambassador?"

"No problem," said Stogie. "But what about Gloria?"

"Uh-uh."

"She was that bad?" asked Stogie, as Gloria walked through the doorway of the tent.

"Max," said Flint wearily, unaware of her presence, "she can't even get a pie in the face without screwing up."

The girl who was no longer Butterfly Delight silently left the tent and went to her room, where she made three rather singular discoveries: she didn't disagree with Flint, she was all out of bitterness, and she had no tears left.

10.

"Jesus H. Christ!" exclaimed Flint. "What the hell is *that*?"

"I think," said Mr. Ahasuerus dryly, "that Simba's replacement has arrived."

Flint shook his head in awe. "I wouldn't trade places with Monk for anything in the universe."

The robots were slowly lowering a huge cage from the hold of a small cargo ship. Inside it, pacing, glaring, snarling, was an animal that seemed to be all muscle and sinew and rage. It was perhaps seven hundred pounds, built very long and low to the ground, with an amazingly flexible spine and powerful haunches that seemed made for springing long distances in very little time. Its eyes were red, its nose broad, its teeth huge and multitudinous, as if layered. It possessed four legs and a short tail that seemed to act more as a rudder than a balance. It was bright red, and covered with very rough scales. At first and even second glance, Flint couldn't decide if it was canine, feline, or reptilian; it simply wasn't like anything he had ever seen before.

"What does it eat—besides lion tamers, that is?" he asked at last.

"I'm sure Kargennian sent along a supply of food, as well as instructions to our galley robots," replied Mr. Ahasuerus. "A fascinating animal. Note the retractable claws, Mr. Flint."

"Note the lion trainer, Mr. Ahasuerus," replied Flint, nodding in Monk's direction.

Jupiter Monk was standing, hands on hips, staring at the animal with a practiced eye. The burly trainer stood motionless for a few minutes, then turned to Flint.

"This is someone's idea of a joke, right?" he said at last.

"Maybe," agreed Flint. "But it's a joke we're stuck with."

"I'll bet every penny I've got that no one has ever trained one of those babies," said Monk fervently.

"What makes you so sure?" asked Flint. "After all, you've only seen him for a couple of minutes, and just in a cage."

"That's just the way I plan to keep on seeing him," said Monk. "That son of a bitch is built for quickness, Thaddeus."

"With all that bulk?" replied Flint dubiously. "I think he'd run out of gas inside a quarter of a mile."

"I didn't say *speed*," said Monk. "I said *quickness*. Look how flexible he is, how balanced. And those front feet—they're made for reaching out and holding things, not just for swatting them."

"So are a lion's."

"Not so," said Monk. "A lion'll swat an antelope's neck and break it. He doesn't have to be accurate. This bastard *catches* things with those paws. What's the return policy on him?"

"Well, the ship's still here," said Flint. "Do you want to put him right back on?"

Monk stared at the creature for a long moment. "I gotta have *something* else for the act. Maybe if I give him a few days to calm down . . ." His voice trailed off. "Can we still return him in a week or two?"

"We can try," said Flint doubtfully.

"Okay, that's what we'll do," said Monk. "Has it got a name?"

"Individually or generically?" inquired Mr. Ahasuerus, who had remained silent up to that point.

"Either one."

"I've seen holographs of this type of creature before," said the blue man, "and I believe I've seen its skeleton in a museum on Lodin XI. The name is unpronounceable to you, but it translates, roughly, as Demoncat."

92

"There's not that much catlike about it," said Monk.

"Of course, I could be wrong," admitted Mr. Ahasuerus. "If you'd like, I can put it through the ship's computer and translator."

"Not necessary," said Monk, never taking his eyes from the beast. "Red Devil's as good a name as any."

"I believe it translates as *Demoncat*," corrected Mr. Ahasuerus.

"Fine," said Monk, walking to within a few feet of the cage. "Red Devil it is."

"But—" began the blue man.

"Shut up, Mr. Ahasuerus," interrupted Flint. "He's the one who's got to get into the cage with it. The least we can do is let him name it."

"But he's wrong," persisted Mr. Ahasuerus.

"I'll tell you what," said Flint with a smile. "You train it, and you can give it any goddamned name you like."

The blue man looked at the beast for a few seconds, then turned back to Flint and exposed his teeth.

"Red Devil it is," he agreed.

"Good. That's over with." Flint stepped aside as the robots carried the cage by and fell into step behind Monk, who led them off to where he kept his animals.

Then, once the beast was a safe distance away, the aliens began to disembark. There were three members of Kargennian's rotund reddish race, and a dozen assorted others, about two-thirds of them humanoid in shape.

Finally one alien, a portly three-legged creature, separated himself from the group and approached Flint.

"Excuse me, sir," he said, "but I was told to report to—"

"Never mind that shit," Flint broke in. "Where the hell are my rides?"

"Rides, sir?" repeated the alien blankly.

"Yeah, my rides. You know—Ferris wheels, stuff like that."

The alien looked confused. "I'm afraid I have no idea, sir. Can you tell me where I may find Mr. Thaddeus Flint?"

"You're looking at him," said Flint, craning his neck to try to see inside the hold. "Were there any big boxes or crates marked for Procyon III?"

"I really couldn't say, sir. I kept to my quarters for most of the voyage."

Flint turned to the blue man. "Get on board and make sure he shipped the rides."

Mr. Ahasuerus sighed, nodded his head, and climbed aboard the ship.

"Okay, friend," said Flint, turning back to the alien, "why don't you and all your pals mosey on over to the Midway? I'll join you in a few minutes and we'll get to work teaching you the games."

The alien remained standing where he was, while his companions milled restlessly in the vicinity of the landing field.

"Well?" demanded Flint harshly.

"Excuse me, sir," said the alien, "but I do not know any of them."

"Then how the hell do you work with them?"

"I don't. I am a magician."

"You?" said Flint unbelievingly.

The alien reached out a stubby hand, and suddenly a bouquet of flowers appeared in it. "Me," he replied.

"Hard to imagine you in a tuxedo and top hat," said Flint, "but what the hell—I guess we'll have to make do. How is it that you speak English?"

"I took an intensive sleep-therapy course on the voyage here. Languages are one of my specialties, sir."

"Someday you must tell me what your other specialties are," replied Flint dryly.

"Well, sir, I—"

"Not just now, Houdini."

"My name is Martthlplexorp," said the alien.

"Not anymore, it isn't," replied Flint.

"Have you some reason for choosing the name Houdini, sir?"

"Yes," said Flint.

The alien waited for an explanation, then sighed and shrugged when none was forthcoming.

"All right," said Flint. "How the hell do I communicate with the rest of them?"

"I assume they all have translators," replied Houdini. "I know I was given one."

Flint, followed by Houdini, walked over to where the aliens were milling around and whistled for attention.

"Can everyone understand me?" he asked.

They all looked blankly at him.

He pulled a translator out of his belt and held it up. "Does anyone have one of these?"

He received nothing but curious expressions.

"Figures," he muttered. "The son of a bitch only gave it to the one guy who didn't need it."

By dint of hand signals and facial expressions, he managed to make them understand that they were to follow him to the games area, where Diggs was waiting. Once there, he hunted up fourteen translating devices and handed them out. Five of them required extensive adjustments before they were of any use to their new owners, but at last everyone signaled that they could understand what he was saying.

"My name is Thaddeus Flint," he announced, "and you are now employees of *The Ahasuerus and Flint Traveling Carnival and Sideshow*. We have very few rules here, but those we have must be obeyed. You don't fight with the customers, you don't leave the grounds without telling myself or Mr. Ahasuerus—he's the blue skeleton who was with me when you landed—where you're going, you never try to cheat the carnival, and you never give a sucker an even break. Got it?"

There was a general murmuring of acquiescence.

"Good. You'll all be quartered on the fourth level of the ship. As soon as I'm through speaking to you you'll have half an hour to go pick out your compartments and unpack any gear you may have brought along. If you've got any special dietary needs, tell the galley robots about it, and may God have mercy on your souls."

He motioned Diggs to step over.

"This gentleman is Jason Oliver Diggs. He likes to be called Diggs. He's in charge of the game booths. When you report back here after selecting your rooms, you will be working directly under him. He'll explain how all the games work, and assign each of you to a booth where he feels you are best suited. I would strongly recommend that you run the games precisely as Diggs tells you to, as he has been known to break a few heads when he feels he's being cheated. Does everyone understand the translation so far?"

He waited for questions, but there were none, and he continued. "Most of you have names that are totally unpronounceable to myself and other members of the carny. Don't worry about it. Sometime in the next couple of days we'll give you all carny names, like my friend Houdini here." He gestured to the alien magician. "Other than that, I strongly advise you not to stick your hands into the cages of any of the animals. Your personal habits are your own business, but you'd better show up clean and sober. That's it."

The aliens wandered off to the ship, and Flint pulled Diggs aside.

"Did you see the big one?" he asked.

"The green one with all the muscles?" grinned the Rigger. "I wonder if you're thinking what I'm thinking?"

"Probably. Find out if he knows how to wrestle."

"Fifty credits to anyone who can last five minutes with him!" laughed Diggs. "Damn! We haven't had a real live wrestler since Sheboygan!"

"Make sure he knows how to use all those muscles first, and then see if he's interested," said Flint. "We'll cut him in for a quarter, but I don't want him out there unless he likes throwing people around. If he's going to be a gentleman, they'll kill him."

"He didn't look all that gentle to me," opined Diggs.

"Well, check it out with him later."

Flint walked over to the cargo ship, where Mr. Ahasuerus was supervising the unloading of a number of plastic crates.

"Any idea what they are yet?" asked Flint.

"Not really," replied the blue man. "We'll have to assemble them first. I'll put the robots to work right away." He paused and looked at the crates. "There's nothing as large as a roller coaster in here, that's for certain."

"Well, then it's a damned good thing Barbara only knows how half the games work, isn't it?" grinned Flint. "I sure wouldn't want the hotshot to think he was taking advantage of us.''

"Son of a bitch!" exclaimed Mr. Ahasuerus.

"Why partner, wherever did you learn to speak like that?" laughed Flint.

11.

The odd-looking magician, still dressed in his flight fatigues, paused in the doorway and cleared his throat. When the girl didn't look up from her book, he coughed a little louder. There was still no response.

"Excuse me," he said at last.

"Who are you?" demanded Gloria, looking up and then jumping to her feet.

"I did not mean to startle you," he said softly. "But I have become confused. Is this the fourth level of the ship?"

She shook her head. "The third. Are you one of the new games workers?"

"I am a magician," he said gravely.

"Really?"

His broad face contorted in a smile. "Is it so hard to believe?"

"Thaddeus didn't mention a magician. What kind of tricks can you do?"

His gaze fell to her vanity, and he picked up a small comb. "May I?" he asked.

She nodded, and he waved his free hand in the air, lowered it slowly over the comb—and suddenly the comb was no longer there.

"That's very good!" said Gloria, smiling. "Where is it?"

"That," replied the alien, returning her smile, "would be telling."

"What's your name?"

"My name is . . ." The magician paused, then started again. "My name is Houdini."

"Of course," laughed Gloria.

"May I inquire who Houdini is?"

"Was," corrected Gloria. "He was the most famous magician in the history of my race."

"Truly?" he asked, and she nodded. "Then I should feel highly complimented." He paused. "May I ask who you are?"

"My name is Gloria."

"And what is your function with the carnival?"

Her face darkened for a moment, then became expressionless. "I take tickets at the specialty tent."

"It sounds . . . fulfilling," said the magician diplomatically.

"Does it now?" said Gloria. "Tell me about yourself, Houdini. Where do you come from?" She walked to her refrigerator. "Can I offer you something to drink?"

"Thank you," he said. "I'm not sure if my metabolism can cope with it, but I've had so many odd things in the past two years I suppose one more won't hurt."

"Fine," she said, withdrawing a pitcher of fruit juice. "Have a seat."

"That, alas, I cannot do," he replied.

"Why not?"

"Your furniture," he explained. "It was not made for beings with a tripodal structure."

She looked at him for a moment, as if seeing him for the first time. "You must forgive me: most of the aliens I've met are so difficult to speak with that when I come across someone like you or Mr. Ahasuerus, I tend to forget that you're really very different from me."

"That's perfectly understandable," said Houdini with a smile. "I must confess that I tend to think of everyone except myself as an alien."

Gloria laughed. "Then, as one alien to another, let me ask you a question: do you *ever* sit down?"

"Oh, yes," replied Houdini. "But while I can adapt to

most gravities and atmosphere contents and foodstuffs, I am afraid that I cannot use any chairs that were not made specifically for my race."

"And what *is* your race?" asked Gloria, pouring a glass of juice and handing it to him.

"I am of the race of Djjong, from the planet of Hesporite III."

She tried pronouncing it a couple of times until he assured her that she had gotten it right.

"How long have you been an entertainer?" she asked.

"Oh, most of my life," replied Houdini, taking a wary sip of the juice. "This is quite good. I think the word is *tart*, is it not?" She nodded, and he continued. "I left Hesporite five years ago to work for the Corporation. I was very glad to hear that I had been transferred here."

"I didn't know we had all that widespread a reputation," commented Gloria dryly.

"You have none at all, although of course word has gone out over the grapevine that your show is somewhat in the nature of an experiment proposed by Mr. Flint under what I understand were rather unusual conditions." He paused. "I have even heard that he held eleven alien tourists hostage until the deal was struck."

"That's not exactly right," said Gloria.

"What a relief to know that he is not the monster he is said to be."

"He was holding them against their wills long before he ever got the idea of joining up with Mr. Ahasuerus," said Gloria.

"But why?"

"He wanted an attraction, and they constituted a ready-made freak show." She smiled. "Don't worry about it. He's mellowed a little since then." Her expression darkened. "Which isn't to say that he can't still be a Grade A bastard when the mood takes him."

"Oh, dear," said Houdini, looking troubled. "I had hoped this place would be different."

"Different from what?" asked Gloria, still having some difficulty viewing him as an alien, rather than an oddly shaped Man.

100

"From the circus. I wasn't very happy there."

"Any particular reason?"

"I had some difficulty making friends," said Houdini.

"You seem like a very friendly sort to me."

"I try to be," said the alien. "I like to think that it was mostly due to resentment."

"Because you were so good at what you did?"

"Because I was so unnecessary," said Houdini with a sigh.

"What do you mean?" asked Gloria, suddenly interested.

"I am a very good magician. I realize that this is an immodest statement, but it is the truth. I have studied and worked at my craft all my life." He paused, reached into the air, and produced Gloria's comb, which he handed back to her. "Most of my tricks are sleight-of-hand. They depend on skill and swiftness and misdirection. I disdain production boxes and other manufactured aids. I feel that a true magician never relies on mechanical contrivances, and so I have never incorporated any into my act."

"I see."

"On Hesporite III, I was acknowledged to be one of the finest magicians of my era. I had a booking agent and a business manager and three assistants, and people appreciated what I did."

"What happened?" asked Gloria, who had a sinking feeling that she knew the answer.

"I had an opportunity to tour the galaxy as a performer with one of the Corporation's shows, which was when I found out that what appeals to one race may arouse no interest at all in another. What good is a mind-reading act in a society of telepaths? Why should a race that possesses the power of telekinesis, that can move objects from one place to another or make them wink out of existence at will, care to see a magician produce flowers out of empty air? What need have they of my illusions?" He paused, lost in thought, for a moment. "I was sent from one show to another, seeking an appreciative audience. At Kargennian's circus I was actually relegated to the role of cleaning up after the animals—but of course I still have a number of years to run on my initial contract, and so I was perhaps the highest-paid lackey in the

101

show, which caused considerable resentment. That's why I was so hopeful when Mr. Flint actually requested a magician. Of course, I found out later that his first choice was a juggler. But my hands are rather deft and facile; perhaps I can learn to juggle if my illusions do not please him.''

"You'll do no such thing!" said Gloria hotly. "You're a magician: *be* a magician!"

"But if Mr. Flint doesn't—"

"Mr. Flint has ruined enough careers!" she continued. "You go out and do what you're best at."

Houdini stared at her for a long moment, his face alien and inscrutable.

"May I assume," he said at last, "that you were not always a ticket-taker?"

"You may."

"Would it be indiscreet to ask what your specialty may have been?"

"No, it's not indiscreet," said Gloria. "I just don't want to talk about it. It's over."

"As you wish. I understand," he said, changing the subject, "that we are to be leaving Procyon III shortly."

Gloria nodded. "I heard something to that effect. I think the only reason we're still here is because we were waiting for you."

"And where will we be going next?"

"It doesn't really matter. One world is pretty much like the next."

"Oh, no!" he said enthusiastically. "You are mistaken. Each, no matter how similar in appearance, has certain intangibles that make it unique. Have you ever been to Altair VIII?"

She shook her head.

"Bareimus III? No? How about—"

"I've been on five ugly little worlds, each more primitive than the last," interrupted Gloria.

"Then you have much to look forward to," said Houdini. "Just within the Community of Worlds itself there are more than three thousand populated planets. Have you ever heard of Vasor?"

"No, I haven't."

"A fabulous world! It's populated by a race of incredibly long-legged beings who spend their entire lives following the sun over the horizon. They never pause to rest, they never know nightfall, they—"

"They also don't have any use for a carnival, do they?" she interrupted.

"No, I suppose not," replied Houdini. "But with so many wondrous worlds at your disposal, you can't view them only in the light of whether or not they would support a carnival."

"Why not? I'm stuck with the show. If it doesn't go there, *I* don't go there."

"But surely you don't plan to remain with the carnival forever," he persisted. "Once your contract runs out—"

"We can't go back to Earth," said Gloria. "Earth isn't a member of your Community. It's not even supposed to know that you exist. So I'm stuck here. These people may not be much, but they're all I've got."

"I see," said the magician slowly.

"*You* can go home, where people appreciate what you do," continued Gloria bitterly. "*I* can't."

There was an awkward silence, during which Houdini sipped thoughtfully at his drink. Finally he looked at her and spoke again. "Can you tell me something about the other specialty acts with which I shall be working?"

"Well, there's Jupiter Monk. You may have seen him, since he was supposed to be having some kind of animal delivered. He's a big guy with a handlebar mustache."

"He *requested* a Demoncat?" asked Houdini unbelievingly.

"I don't know the story on it," replied Gloria. "All I know is that he came out with four animals, and one of them has already died. He needed a replacement."

"It happens," agreed the magician. "Animals seem to have a much harder time making adjustments to new worlds than do sentient beings."

"The other one is Billybuck Dancer. You probably won't see him until showtime. He keeps pretty much to himself."

"And what is his area of expertise?"

"He's a sharpshooter."

"I'm afraid the term is unfamiliar to me."

"How can I put it?" said Gloria. "He has this gun that shoots bullets . . ."

"Ah! A projectile weapon!"

"I guess so. Anyway, he can shoot a cigarette out of your mouth at one hundred feet. He also throws knives."

"It sounds fascinating," said Houdini. "I must be sure to watch his performance."

"He's pretty good," admitted Gloria. "A little crazy, but good."

"Crazy?" repeated Houdini with a worried expression.

"Oh, he doesn't go around shooting people," said Gloria with an amused smile, "if that's what you're worrying about. He's just a bit . . . well, *odd*. You always get the feeling that he's not really listening to you, that his mind is somewhere else."

"It's all very confusing," answered the magician, "but I'm sure I'll be highly entertained."

"Most people are."

"I wonder if I could make one further imposition upon you," said Houdini hesitantly.

"I don't know," said Gloria. "What is it?"

"Mr. Flint seems to have left me totally on my own, while he is concentrating on helping Diggs train the new staff for the game booths. Since the nature of your job is such that you do not have to spend long hours practicing at it, I wonder if you might show me around." He looked hopefully at her. "I really don't know who else to ask."

She shrugged. "Sure. Why not?"

"Good!" he exclaimed. "I will go to the fourth level and claim a compartment, and then return for you."

"I'll be here," said Gloria.

He walked to the door, then turned briefly to face her. "You have been very kind to me. I hope that you will become my friend."

"You sound like you could use one," she replied.

She waited until he had left, then added under her breath: "Almost as much as me."

12.

John Edward Carp locomoted—*there is no other word for it*—through the muck and the slime that had become his home, exulting in the feel of his undulating musculature, the rich texture of the oxygen coursing through his bloodstream, the pungent odors that existed nowhere else in the galaxy.

Though he no longer had eyes, he saw—*again, no other word will suffice*—three of his companions huddled about a small puddle, sucking sustenance from it.

"Greetings, John Edward Carp," burbled the nearest of the three. "May strength and health permeate your essence."

Carp attempted an obeisance that he had not yet fully mastered, and returned the salutation.

"Have they contacted you yet?"

"No," answered Carp.

"They will. The ship is valuable. Soon they will come for it—and for you."

Carp wrinkled his vast gray nostrils contemptuously.

"Let 'em," he replied.

13.

"Back off!" shouted Monk.

The entire crew of the carnival, which had crowded around the training cage to watch Monk's first encounter with the Red Devil, backed away.

"Farther! I don't want him getting the idea that he's surrounded."

The carnival had left the Procyonian system forty-eight hours after the aliens' arrival, but instead of going directly to Mirzam X, the next planet on its agenda, it had diverted to Belore II when Monk insisted upon a gravity identical to Earth's for his first few sessions with the beast.

"What makes you think he'll like Earth gravity?" Flint had protested. "We don't even know what kind of world he comes from."

"Maybe not," Monk had answered firmly. "But I know what kind of world *I* come from—and if I've got to jump or sidestep to save my life, I want my feet to wind up where I was planning for them to wind up."

Flint had argued futilely, and finally had Mr. Ahasuerus arrange a six-day booking on Belore II, which, with 98.3% Earth gravity, was the closest Monk was likely to get to his ideal conditions.

Actually, thought Flint as the Red Devil's cage was wheeled out and buttressed up against the door of the training cage, the trip to Belore might work out all the way around. While Monk was working with the animal, he and Diggs would turn it into a shakedown period for the new crew, learning their strengths and weaknesses and figuring out what to do about the latter.

"Careful!" snapped Monk to the two robots that were handling the cage. "Don't get him riled up."

Then the door slid open, and suddenly the Red Devil leaped to the center of the training cage with incredible swiftness.

"Jesus, he's quick!" muttered Monk from his position just outside the door.

Flint approached him. "You sure you want to go through with this? He looks a lot bigger here than in his own cage."

"Might as well," said Monk grimly. "I ain't getting any younger and he ain't getting any nicer." He turned to the crowd until he spotted the man he was looking for. "Hey, Dancer!"

The Dancer approached him. "Want me to ride shotgun, Jupiter?" he asked pleasantly.

"Something like that," admitted Monk. "Stay close to the door and put a bullet into this bastard if it looks like I'm in trouble."

"I'd say you were in a mess of trouble already," offered the Dancer.

"I agree," said Flint. "Jupiter, let's call this whole thing off and send the goddamned animal back gift-wrapped to Kargennian."

Monk sighed and shook his head. "I'm an animal trainer, Thaddeus. This is my job. It's what you pay me to do."

"I'm not paying you enough to mess with *that* thing," said Flint fervently.

"If it comes to that, Thaddeus," said Monk with a smile, "you ain't paying me enough to mess with Bruno or the leopards, either."

He withdrew his whip from his belt, picked up a small metal chair with his left hand, and walked to the door.

"Dancer, go around the other side and get his attention for a minute," he said.

The Dancer walked halfway around the cage and stepped

107

up to the bars. The result was electrifying: the Red Devil leaped across the intervening distance in a single bound, shot a forepaw between the bars, and missed taking off the Dancer's face by less than an inch.

"That's some pet you've got, Jupiter," said the Dancer, more amused than startled.

Monk didn't answer. He had stepped inside the cage and was waiting for the robots to lock the door before calling the beast's attention to himself. When he heard the catch click into place he whistled once, then held the chair out in front of him as the Red Devil turned to face him.

The huge carnivore crouched as if to spring again, and Monk cracked his whip. The sound caused the Red Devil to flinch, and it jumped some ten feet to its right.

"Quick," muttered Monk, not without a touch of admiration. "Goddamned quick!"

He stood motionless for a few seconds, waiting to see what the Red Devil would do next. When the beast contented itself with glaring at him, he took a step forward, extending the chair in front of him. Nothing happened, and he took another step.

Then the Red Devil roared and charged at him. He backed up two paces, and the creature came to a stop twelve feet from him.

He knew he'd made a mistake. The next time the Red Devil tried to bluff him it would assume he was going to back away, and if he didn't, they were likely to collide more by accident than design.

He cracked the whip again and took a step toward the beast, hoping to make it back away. It didn't move, and he extended the arm that was holding the chair and took another step—and, with a suddenness that surprised him even though he was expecting it, the Red Devil bounded forward and slapped at the chair with a forepaw. It was ripped out of his hand, and careened off the bars some fifteen feet away.

"Now?" asked the Dancer.

Monk shook his head, afraid that the sound of his voice might startle the creature and precipitate a charge.

They stood motionless, glaring at each other, for the better part of thirty seconds. Then Monk's gaze fell on one of the stools he used for the leopards, and he decided to see if he could drive the Red Devil over to it. He cracked the whip once to get the creature's attention riveted upon it, then snaked it out and snapped it again.

The Red Devil hissed and backed away. Monk circled around it, always keeping the whip between them, until he reached the chair. Never taking his eyes from the creature, he leaned down and retrieved it. Not that the chair would afford him any protection, but it would give the Red Devil an extra target, and might buy him the fraction of a second he needed to avoid an all-out attack if one was launched.

He started muttering words, meaningless words to get the creature used to the sound of his voice. The Red Devil hissed and snarled and crouched as if to charge, but then the whip cracked again and once more it backed off.

Monk approached a little closer, then started swaying back and forth to make it harder for the creature to gauge his distance. Finally it was the constant motion itself that precipitated another charge, and this time Monk snapped the whip against the Red Devil's moist, leathery nostrils.

The creature roared in pain and surprise, and jumped completely across the cage before turning to face Monk once again.

"So now you know it does more than make noise," whispered Monk. "Now let's see if you're smart enough to avoid it."

He began cracking the whip to the left side of the Red Devil, hoping to move it to the right. It took two steps to the right, then stood motionless while the whip touched it again.

Then, without a sound, it hurled itself straight at the animal trainer. Monk held the chair out, only to see it go flying across the cage again. He flicked out the whip, but the Red Devil paid it no attention. It stalked him, belly to ground, soundlessly, oblivious to the noise and pain of the whip, and Monk began backing away toward the door.

Suddenly the Red Devil leaped right past him and positioned itself by the door, and Monk began backing away in the opposite direction.

And now the stalk continued, as the creature, silent as

Death, its red eyes gleaming, slowly approached the trainer, no longer even pretending to notice the whip.

"Get ready, Dancer!" said Monk sharply.

The Red Devil backed him up against the bars, then slowly, almost leisurely, gathered itself to pounce upon him. Monk yelled and took a single step toward it, hoping to scare it back, but it paid no notice whatsoever.

Then a single shot rang out, and all hell broke loose. The Red Devil screamed, careened over backward, and started clawing at the canvas floor. Finally it looked up at Monk and hurled itself at him, and the Dancer fired again.

The creature did a full flip in the air and began turning in circles, totally disoriented. Three more quick shots finally put it on its side, and then the Dancer entered the cage and put a final bullet through the Red Devil's eye. It shuddered once and then lay still.

"Not much stopping power in a cowboy pistol," said the Dancer apologetically.

Monk was too weak and breathless to answer. He stood where he was, propped up against the bars of the cage, until his heart stopped pounding. Then, finally, he took a deep breath, let it out, and walked to the door.

"I'm sorry, Thaddeus," he said as Flint approached him.

"About what?" asked Flint, honestly bewildered.

"I cost you an animal." He turned back and looked at the Red Devil. "Lord, he was something! I never saw anything that big move that fast. And smart! He was just playing games the whole time I was trying to work him with my whip."

"You almost sound as if you liked him," said Houdini, stepping forward to get a better look at the dead animal.

"No one could like something like *that*," said Monk. "But I sure as hell respected him. Still do, for that matter. Lord, he was quick!" He shrugged. "Well, I guess it's back to the leopards and bears. I'd sure like to meet the guy who puts a Red Devil through its paces."

"No one ever has," said Houdini.

"Somehow that doesn't surprise me," said Monk. He turned to Flint. "Thaddeus, I want another one."

"What the hell are you talking about?" demanded Flint.

"I want another Red Devil. If the show won't pay for it, take it out of my salary. I've got no place to spend it anyway."

"Are you crazy?" said Flint. "You were in there with it. You saw what it's like."

"Thaddeus," said Monk patiently, "I'm an animal trainer. It's what I am, it's what I do. This is an animal that's never been tamed. I can't keep fucking around with bears and leopards after being in there with something like a Red Devil."

"You're nuts, you know that?" snapped Flint. "What would have happened if the Dancer's aim had been off?"

"I don't want the Dancer around next time. I'll take other precautions—precautions that won't wind up killing it."

"We'll talk about it tomorrow," said Flint, "after your brain starts functioning again."

"I'm gonna tell you the same thing tomorrow," answered Monk. Flint snorted and walked off, and the animal trainer turned to Houdini. "Do you know a lot about these animals?"

"Very little, actually," replied the magician. "I've seen two on display in zoos, and of course Kargennian exhibited this one for almost a year."

"I've got to shower and grab some lunch and work out with my animals," said Monk, "but I want to talk to you later. How's dinnertime suit you?"

"Fine," said Houdini. "But I must agree with Mr. Flint. Only a person bent on suicide would want a second encounter with a Demoncat."

"Maybe," said Monk. "But if I let one of these bastards scare me, then pretty soon I'll be afraid to work with Bruno and the cats. An animal trainer who's lost his guts ain't an animal trainer anymore. You follow me?"

"I am trying to," admitted Houdini. "But I think there is a fallacy in your reasoning."

"I'm not talking about being right!" snapped Monk. "I'm talking about being *me*!" He smiled and shrugged. "I didn't mean to yell at you. Keep dinnertime open, okay?"

"All right," said the magician with a sigh.

Monk walked off to the ship, and the crew began dispersing. Houdini saw Gloria walking away and hurried ahead to join her.

"It was quite exciting, wasn't it?" he asked her.

"He was almost killed," she replied coldly. "Is that your idea of excitement?"

"Well, to be honest, yes," admitted Houdini. "I mean, isn't that the underlying reason why people come to see him—the thought that he *might* be killed?"

"If you say so."

"You seem unhappy. Is it something I have said or done?"

"No, Houdini. Can't a person be unhappy over something you're not responsible for?"

They wandered to a lichen-covered knoll about a quarter of a mile from the ship and sat down in the shade of a large, treelike fern possessed of huge yellow leaves.

"It has something to do with Monk," said Houdini, finally breaking the silence.

"Nosy, aren't you?"

"I don't mean to be, but you're the only person here who has taken an interest in me, so naturally I am distressed that you are unhappy. You have some emotional attachment toward Monk and were afraid that the animal would kill him."

"Toward Jupiter?" she laughed. "Don't be silly!"

"Then perhaps it is the fact that he will very likely be throwing away his life the next time he steps into a cage with a Demoncat."

She shook her head. "It's *what* he'll be throwing his life away for."

"You object to animal training?"

"I object to the fact that he'll be allowed to give everything, even his life, for his art, and that I am allowed to give nothing. Now do you understand?"

"Ah, yes!" he said, his features brightening perceptibly. "I believe I do."

"By this time you ought to. You've been tagging around after me like a puppy these past three days."

"Does it offend you?" he asked, suddenly solicitous.

"No," she sighed. "I suppose not."

She pulled a few pieces of lichen out of the ground and

began rolling them idly between her fingers while looking off toward the horizon.

"Gloria?" Houdini said hesitantly after a few minutes had passed.

"Yes?"

"I heard someone mention this morning that you were a stripper."

"So now you know."

"Not really," he replied apologetically. "I know that you were one, but I don't know what a stripper *does*."

"You're putting me on," she said disbelievingly.

"Truly I am not."

"A stripper disrobes to musical accompaniment."

"I see," said Houdini. "And then what?"

"What do you mean—*then what*? That's it."

"Perhaps I misunderstood you," said the magician. "You're saying that what you do is take off your clothes while music plays?"

She looked at him wearily. "Doesn't do much for you, does it?"

"There must be more to it than that. After all, how long can it take to disrobe? Five seconds? Ten? Surely not thirty."

"Sometimes it took as much as twenty minutes," said Gloria with a wistful smile.

"I *knew* it was more complex than you made it seem!" said Houdini triumphantly. "Did you sing?"

She shook her head, still smiling. "No. I didn't tell jokes or recite poetry or do magic tricks, either."

Gloria thought his face had become less human and more alien again, as he tried to envision someone taking twenty minutes merely to climb out of her clothes.

"Well, whatever you did, I am certain there was an art to it," he said diplomatically.

"There was," said Gloria.

He was silent for a long minute. Then he looked up brightly. "You juggled!"

"No," she laughed. "Not even that."

"Then . . ." He shrugged and let his voice trail off.

"All right," she said. "You're just going to make an ass of yourself asking Monk or someone else if I don't explain it to you." He smiled gratefully at her, and she continued. "I notice that you wear clothing. Is that common to your race, or do you do it because the other members of the carnival do?"

"All the Djjongi wear clothing," he replied.

"Only for warmth?"

"No," he said. "We control our environment, like almost all civilized races."

"Then why?"

"Custom," he said. "And religious strictures."

"Does anyone ever go naked in your society?"

He shook his head. "Only infants, and then only in the privacy of their homes."

"I have been assuming all along that you are a male, but this seems like a proper time to ask: are you?"

"Most definitely," he assured her.

"What would your reaction be to seeing an unclad female of your race?"

"Shock," he replied promptly. Then he considered the matter for a moment. "And shame," he added.

"And sexual excitement?" asked Gloria.

"Please," he stammered. "This is not a fit topic for discussion."

"Then it *would* excite you?"

"Possibly," he answered aloofly.

"Possibly, hell!" laughed Gloria. "It would drive you right up a wall, you dirty old man!"

"I hope you have a reason for embarrassing me," he said uncomfortably.

"I'm not trying to embarrass you. I'm explaining what I do. I disrobe, as sensually and suggestively as I can, to music."

"In front of males of your race?" he demanded, visibly shocked.

"And an occasional kinky female."

"And do you then perform—how shall I say it—the act of propagation with them?"

"No. The purpose of stripping is simply to titillate."

"I've never heard of anything like that!" exclaimed Houdini.

"Neither, it seems, has anyone else in this goddamned galaxy."

"Aren't you horribly embarrassed when you perform?" he persisted.

"Of course not. It's my job—or anyway, it *was* my job."

He lowered his head in thought, toying absentmindedly with some fronds that had fallen near him. Finally he looked up. "It is a unique concept, I will grant you that. Is it very popular on your world?"

"Less and less," admitted Gloria.

"Stricter morality?" he asked.

"Just the opposite."

"But—?"

"Once upon a time, the only place you could see a naked woman outside your own bedroom, or maybe the *National Geographic*—that's a magazine—was in a strip show. Now that's all changed. Every actress we have has taken her clothes off. The magazines are filled with nudes. The beaches are covered with naked people. Women wear see-through dresses. All strippers do is tease; Linda Lovelace delivers."

"Linda—?"

"An actress, of sorts. No, to be truthful, time and morality have kind of passed strippers by. That's why I came out here: I thought I could keep on doing what I wanted to do, what I'm good at." She shrugged. "I was wrong."

"Possibly you haven't played the proper world yet," he said comfortingly.

"There *is* no proper world for me," she said. "*You* can't be a magician on worlds where they have psi powers. Well, *I* can't be a stripper anywhere but Earth." She looked at him. "What would you do if I took off my shirt right now?"

"Nothing. Why?"

"What would you do if a Djjong lady took off her shirt five feet away from you?"

He turned away and fumbled for an answer.

"See what I mean?" she said.

"Yes," he admitted uncomfortably. "But still, it seems to me that an art form that incorporates dance and music should be able to find an appreciative audience on its own merits somewhere."

"The art is to elicit a biological response by virtue of the dance," she replied. "That sort of limits the audience, doesn't it?"

"I agree. But why be a stripper at all?"

"Why are you a magician?" she shot back.

"I do it well, and it makes me happy," said Houdini.

"Ditto."

"There must be a world for you somewhere," he said.

"There is," replied Gloria. "I walked out on it." She paused. "Anyway, now you know why I'm upset about Monk. It isn't that he's going to throw his life away in the ring with a Demoncat. It's that he's got something to throw his life away *for*."

They sat in silence for a few more minutes, then rose and prepared to return to the ship.

"Just a minute, Gloria," said Houdini.

She turned to him, and he moved his hands mystically in the air. Suddenly he muttered a pair of odd-sounding words, and produced a small bouquet of colorful flowers.

"For you," he said, extending his hand.

"Thank you," said Gloria, taking the proffered gift. "It's been a long time since anyone gave me flowers. For a snoopy little alien who's doing what he wants for a living, you're not such a bad apple at that."

"May I assume that is a compliment?" asked Houdini, beaming.

"Assume anything you want," said Gloria, holding the flowers up to her face and hoping he didn't see the tear that trickled down her cheek.

14.

It was three in the morning, the show was shut down for the night, and Flint sat in the mess hall, sharing his rapidly diminishing stock of beer with Diggs, Monk, and Tojo. The only other person in the room was Billybuck Dancer, who sat alone at a table in the corner, staring off into time and space, totally oblivious to the argument that was taking place at Flint's table.

"Thaddeus, that's the worst damned carny name I ever heard of!" exclaimed Diggs.

Flint popped open another can and grinned at him.

"He wears a toga, doesn't he?"

"So what?" demanded Diggs.

"And he's got green skin, just like a snake—and he wins most of his matches with a bear hug," added Flint.

"I know. But *Julius Squeezer*, for Christ's sake!"

"You got a better name?"

"No," admitted Diggs. "But I'd sure be hard pressed to come up with a worse one."

"The guy's won thirty-one out of thirty-three matches: he deserves a carny name," said Flint firmly. "Hell, I'd invite him to join us for a beer, but I imagine he's gotta keep in training." He turned to the hunchback. "Tojo, that's how I want you to announce him starting tomorrow."

"Julius Squeezer it is," said Tojo wearily.

"While we're on the subject of names," Monk put in, "maybe we ought to change Stogie's to the Pied Piper. Have you seen the way the crowds have been following him out from town the past couple of weeks?"

"Never would have thought the old boy had it in him," admitted Diggs. "Still, at—what?—two thousand extra a night, hell, he must be responsible for thirty thousand admissions just since we touched down on Mirzam X. And he pulled about ten thousand back on that world where you killed the Red Devil. What was its name?"

"Belore," said Flint. "You know, Rigger, sometimes I think your memory's starting to go."

"I remember the important stuff," Diggs shot back. "Like how to fleece a mark. We took in almost a quarter of a million credits tonight."

"I know," said Flint. "And the rides picked up forty thousand more."

"Some rides!" snorted Monk. "They make a merry-go-round look wild by comparison."

"Yeah," said Flint. "But these people have never even seen a merry-go-round. As long as we're making money with them, that's all that counts."

"We've turned things around, that's for sure," said Diggs. "I've got a good feeling about the rest of the tour, Thaddeus."

"You'd sure as hell better," replied Flint with a smile. "It's not as if you can go home if you're unhappy."

"Who wants to go home?" persisted Diggs. "Maybe now that we're making money, we can finally get out of the sticks and hit a couple of interesting worlds."

"If there are any," said Flint sardonically.

"Oh, there are," Diggs said with assurance. "Any worlds that produced some of the aliens I've got working the games *have* to be interesting."

"Any word on Fast Johnny yet?" said Monk.

Flint shrugged. "Not a peep. And the son of a bitch has still got our ship. I suppose I'm going to have to go out after him one of these days, if I can ever learn to pilot one of the two-man jobs."

"Mr. Ahasuerus says the piloting is easy," offered Tojo. "It's the navigation that's difficult."

"Whatever," said Flint.

"Thaddeus . . ." began Monk hesitantly.

"Yeah?"

"Let *me* go out after him."

"What the hell for?"

"I gotta hunt up some animals," said Monk. "I haven't wanted to bring it up with everything going so well, but both the cats have diarrhea."

"The food?" asked Flint.

"Who the hell knows? We've been using synthesized food for the past two months. We ran out of real meat back on Kligor." He paused, staring at his beer can. "I think I'm gonna lose them pretty soon."

"I'm sorry to hear that, Jupiter," said Flint. "But what makes you think some animal you capture on one of these planets can take the routine any better than they could?"

"It'll take more than a little traveling to kill one of those Red Devils," said Monk fervently.

"And it'll take more than one guy who doesn't even know where they come from to capture one," replied Flint firmly. "Besides, you know the score on them: they've never been tamed. You'd either have to kill it or give up on it, and then you'd just be going off to hunt up another one." He shook his head. "No, now that we've turned the corner, I think I can get the Corporation to supply us with whatever animals you need."

"Whatever they send, it'll be something people have seen before. There's a million worlds out there that haven't been touched, Thaddeus," said Monk, his eyes shining. "Let me go out there and bring back something no one's ever laid eyes on!"

"And by the time you get what you're after, Fast Johnny will have died of old age and his ship will be buried in some swamp," said Flint with a smile. "I can't okay it, Jupiter. Let's see what else we can come up with."

"All right," sighed Monk. "But it better be fast. Those poor cats are gonna be dehydrated in another week or two." He stared across the table at Flint. "And I ain't about to spend the rest of my life holding up targets for the Dancer."

"Nobody's asking you to," said Flint. "Do you want me to try to get a vet for the cats?"

"I spoke with Mr. Ahasuerus about it," said Monk. "He tells me that by the time they analyze what makes 'em tick, they'll probably be dead. So I guess I'll just tend to them the best I can, and hope I can pull them through it—this time."

"You expect them to get sick again?" asked Tojo.

"These things ain't housecats, Tojo," said Monk. "They're hard enough to keep alive in zoos. If a leopard makes up his mind to die, the best vet in the world ain't gonna talk him out of it."

"How's Bruno doing?" asked Flint.

"Mean as ever. But he ain't exactly the smartest bear that ever lived. It took me five years to drill five minutes' worth of tricks into that pea-sized brain of his. There's no way I'm ever going to fill a twenty-minute act with just him. Besides," he added with a smile, "we're not real fond of each other."

"I'll have Mr. Ahasuerus get in touch with Kargennian and see what he can arrange."

"Okay—but I'd still like to go out there and hunt up my own animals."

Flint shook his head. "No way. I can't put the Dancer on for a whole hour."

"How about Houdini?" persisted Monk.

"He's good for seven minutes, tops," said Flint. He looked toward the airlock, where the magician was just entering the ship. "Speaking of the devil . . ."

"Good evening, Mr. Flint," said Houdini, walking toward the elevator. "Gentlemen."

"What are you doing up so late?" asked Flint.

"I was helping Gloria balance her receipts at the specialty tent, sir."

"You mean she's *still* working on them?" demanded Flint unbelievingly.

"Actually, we were talking," replied Houdini. "I wasn't aware that there was a deadline."

"There's not," said Flint. "Well, don't just stand there looking awkward. Pull up a chair and have a beer."

120

"I thank you for the invitation, sir," said the magician, "but my metabolism cannot cope with alcohol."

"Better and better," said Flint. "Come join us anyway."

"I would like to, sir," said Houdini, "but I'm afraid that I cannot use your chairs."

"Then come on over and *don't* pull up a chair," said Flint irritably.

"Thank you, sir," said Houdini, walking across the mess hall and joining them. "Should I asked Billybuck Dancer to join us also?"

"Leave him alone," said Monk. "He's busy shooting it out with Doc Holliday."

"I am afraid I don't understand."

"Don't worry about it," said Monk. "He's happy where he is."

"So," said Flint, "how do you like carny life so far?"

"It's quite different from Kargennian's circus, sir."

"In what way? And stop calling me sir."

"Yes, sir," replied Houdini. "I find that everyone here is more involved in things. You all seem to take a vital interest in the success of the operation."

"That's because we ain't got anyplace to go if it folds," said Monk with a smile. "You sure you won't have a beer? Thaddeus loves to give it away."

"Really, I cannot," said the magician.

"By the way," added Monk, "I've been meaning to tell you— I've caught your act a few times, and you're pretty damned good."

"Thank you very much, sir," replied Houdini.

"That sounds kind of nice," laughed Monk. "You can call *me* sir whenever the mood takes you."

"*I* haven't seen your act yet," said Diggs. "Just how good are you?"

"I try my best, sir," said Houdini. "That's all I can tell you."

"No false modesty around here," said Monk. "Like I said, you're good."

Diggs pulled a deck of cards out of his pocket. "Ever do any tricks with these things, Houdini?"

The magician shook his head. "Gloria has told me to borrow a deck and start learning how to do tricks with them, but so far I haven't found the time."

121

"Nothing to it," grinned Diggs. "Pick a card."

Houdini pulled a card and looked at it.

"Got it memorized?" asked Diggs. "Good. Now put it back."

Houdini replaced the card, and Diggs shuffled the deck thoroughly. "Now pick a number from one to ten,"

"Seven," said Houdini.

Diggs gave the deck one final shuffle, then dealt out six cards and turned the seventh one up.

"Is that it?" he asked.

"Yes, it is!" exclaimed Houdini. "Now I know why Gloria wanted me to learn card tricks. That was very impressive, sir!"

"Just Diggs will do. Or Rigger, if you prefer. Here," he added, handing the deck to Houdini. "Let's see what you can do with them."

The magician went through the cards one by one, asking Diggs to identify the court cards and the names of the suits. Then he shuffled them tentatively a couple of times and had Diggs pick a card.

The process was the same, up until the result, at which point the card turned up fourth when the Rigger's number was five.

"I see it will take long hours of practice," said Houdini glumly.

"Don't sell yourself short," said Monk. "For a guy who's never held a deck of cards before, that's damned good work."

"And these are just for tricks?" asked the magician.

"We play games with 'em from time to time," said Diggs, a look of predation passing swiftly over his face. "I don't suppose you'd like to learn one?"

"I should be honored, sir," replied Houdini.

Diggs began explaining the basics of poker, while Tojo leaned over to Flint and whispered: "You've got to stop this, Thaddeus. It's not right to fleece one of our own!"

"View it as a learning experience," whispered Flint with a smile. "I'll stop it if it gets out of hand."

They played three hands of draw, and Diggs lost all three.

"It's really very simple, isn't it, sir?" asked Houdini.

"Diggs. And yes, it is. In fact, sometimes it gets so out-and-out dull that we make little bets, just to amuse ourselves." He cocked an eyebrow. "I don't suppose you'd be interested?"

"Well, as long as it's just a *small* bet . . ."

"Fine," said Diggs with a grin. "Shall we say five credits?"

The magician nodded, and Diggs dealt another hand. Houdini won again, and Diggs doubled the bet. This time Houdini had a straight to the Rigger's two pairs.

"You're getting good at this," said Diggs grudgingly. "Care to double the stakes again?"

"If we do nothing but double them, then sooner or later we're going to wind up even," pointed out the magician. "Why don't I just return your money now?"

"Well, if the thought of breaking even bothers you, we might as well start playing this man-to-man, if you'll pardon the expression."

"I thought we were."

"Well, actually, it's customary to bet at the beginning of the hand and bet again after the draw."

"But why not just determine the amount of the bets and play for that sum?" asked Houdini.

Diggs went on to explain the art of bluffing and of backing one's cards with the coin of the realm, and finally Houdini nodded.

They played three more hands. Diggs won a small pot and Houdini won two rather large ones.

"Well," said Diggs, closing in for the kill, "I seem to be out almost two hundred credits."

"I am sorry," said Houdini. "Again, if you wish, I will simply return your money."

"Why don't we play one last hand?" asked Diggs.

"But you seem to be having such poor luck," said the magician.

"Well, now, luck's a funny thing. It can change on a second's notice."

"Not tonight, Rigger," said Flint, picking up on Diggs' signal.

"The hell it won't!" snapped Diggs.

"Forget it," said Flint. "He's too good for you."

"Screw you, Thaddeus!" snarled Diggs. He turned to face the magician. "We'll play this one for five hundred credits!"

"But—"

"No goddamned carny owner is gonna say that Digger the Rigger's over the hill! Come on, Houdini—put up your money!"

"But I don't have that much with me."

"I'll take your marker."

"My what?" asked the magician.

"If I win, you can owe it to me," said Diggs, reaching into his pocket and slapping five one-hundred-credit notes on the table. "Ready?"

The magician shrugged. "I guess so."

Diggs dealt out the cards, and Flint stood up and walked behind Houdini to see what he had. The magician held four jacks and a two of spades.

"Jacks or better to open?" asked Flint.

"By me," said Diggs. "I can't make it."

"I believe I can," said Houdini. "I feel guilty about this, sir, but I must bet all of my accumulated winnings."

"Damn!" muttered Diggs, reaching into his pocket for another two hundred credits. "All I needed was one decent hand!" He placed the notes on the table. "I'll take three cards," he said, reaching for the deck.

"Excuse me, sir," said Houdini, "but I believe *I* go first."

"Huh? Ain't you standing pat?"

"I do not know the expression," admitted the magician, "but I would like two cards, please." He threw away a jack and the deuce.

"But—"

"My cards, please," said Houdini, smiling pleasantly.

Diggs glared at him silently for a minute, then disgustedly dealt two cards to him.

"Dealer takes three," he announced, taking three cards for himself.

"I believe I have a full house, sir," said Houdini with a

124

smile. He turned over the two cards to reveal a pair of kings. "And you, of course, have a pair of kings—one that you kept and one that you drew."

"Goddamned three-legged card shark!" said Diggs, scowling and throwing his cards onto the table.

Flint and Monk emitted roars of delightful laughter.

"That was a very deftly performed shuffle, sir," said Houdini politely. "I assure you that only a magician would have noticed it."

"Fuck you!" snapped Diggs, shouting to be heard over the laughter.

"I *like* poker," continued Houdini. "It's an invigorating game. Perhaps we can play again tomorrow, and let someone else deal. I really have no desire for your money."

"You keep out of my way for a few days, you hear?" growled Diggs. He stood up. "I'm going to bed."

Flint and Monk were still laughing as he left the mess hall and took the elevator to his room.

"Welcome to the club, Houdini!" said Flint. "If you weren't one of us before, you sure as hell are now!"

"Thank you, sir," replied the magician.

"Are you sure you've never seen a deck of cards before?"

"Well, not with those particular figures and numbers on them," replied Houdini with a smile.

"Houdini," said Monk, "I think you and I are going to be friends. Ain't nobody flim-flammed the Rigger since I done it back on Earth."

"With cards, sir?" asked the magician.

"Nope. Just as well—nobody fools him twice. I'd be real careful if I played him again."

"I shall take your advice to heart," said Houdini sincerely. "I only hope he isn't too mad."

"So what if he is?" said Flint. "He had it coming."

"He'll get over it," put in Tojo. "He just doesn't like to appear foolish in front of his friends."

"I should have probably let him win," said the magician. "It's just that *I* don't like to appear foolish either."

"You're quite a guy, Houdini!" said Flint.

"Thank you, sir."

"God, I love to see the Rigger lose!" continued Flint. "You've made my week."

"Then I wonder if I might ask you a favor, sir."

"Shoot."

"It's not for myself," said Houdini hastily.

Suddenly Flint's face hardened. "If it's for your girlfriend, the answer's no."

"I don't understand the term 'girlfriend,' sir, but I assume you are referring to Gloria."

"I am."

"And you are refusing my request before you even hear it?"

"There is only one thing in the world she wants, and I just can't give it to her."

"But she's so unhappy just taking tickets," persisted Houdini.

"Did she put you up to this?" demanded Flint.

"No!" exclaimed the magician, suddenly upset. "I think she would be quite mad at me for broaching the subject. Please don't tell her about this conversation, sir!"

"I won't," said Flint, his expression softening. "But damn it, Houdini, there's not a thing I can do for her. I met her halfway on Procyon and it wasn't enough."

"Perhaps a world where her art is appreciated . . ." suggested Houdini.

"If there was such a world, I'd make it our next stop just to shut her up. Jesus! Do you think I *enjoy* watching her walk around like Death warmed over?"

"But she has described her act to me, and I must admit that I find it fascinating."

"Would *you* pay money to watch her undress?" said Flint. "If you can truthfully tell me you would, we'll take off for your world tomorrow."

Houdini met his gaze with a troubled expression. "That's not a fair question, sir."

"It's not a fair situation," responded Flint. "What's your answer?"

"No," said Houdini at last. "I wouldn't pay to watch her."

"I know," replied Flint.

"Then is she to spend the rest of her life counting other people's money?"

"It sure as hell looks like it," said Flint, wondering what he had found so side-splittingly funny only a few moments ago.

15.

"Good morning," said Gloria, as Houdini approached her on the lichen-covered knoll. "I'll be with you in a minute."

She finished her last twenty sit-ups, then propped herself up against one of the huge, yellow-leafed ferns and wiped her face with a towel.

"Good morning, Gloria," said the magician. "May I join you?"

"Of course. I hear you got involved in a little card game last night."

"It was nothing."

"That's not the way I heard it. Monk is going around telling anyone who will listen to him how you conned the Rigger."

"It was really a case of the biter getting bitten," replied Houdini with a smile. "Had he not tried to stack the cards against me, I would not have been able to anticipate the nature of his hand."

"Well, Thaddeus is fond of saying that you should never try to bullshit a bullshitter. I guess it applies to card sharps, too," she said, returning his smile. "I'm very proud of you for standing up to them."

"Them?" he repeated, puzzled. "It was only Diggs."

"Nonsense. It was *all* of them, except maybe Tojo."

"The only person I played cards with was Diggs."

"But Thaddeus and Monk knew what he was trying to do to you. They could have warned you."

"It is only natural that they did not. After all, Diggs is one of them. I am not."

"The hell you're not!" she said firmly. "Stop being so self-effacing! You work for the show, don't you? That's the only qualification anyone's ever needed. It's the carnies against the marks."

"Well, they *did* seem delighted that Diggs lost," he admitted thoughtfully. "And even Diggs himself came around this morning to tell me that he bore me no grudge. I offered to give him back his money again, but he refused to accept it—so tonight we are playing a new game called blackjack. I gather that Mr. Flint has agreed to deal, so as to avoid any misunderstandings."

"Keep an eye on him," warned Gloria. "He's almost as good with a deck of cards as Diggs is."

"Really? He is quite a remarkable man. I understand that he is also the best barker the show possesses, and I have been told that he once jumped into the training cage—many years back, to be sure—when Monk was being attacked by a trio of cats. Is that true?"

"I've heard the same story," said Gloria. "I suppose it *is* true—but I always thought it wasn't so much heroism as the thought of losing a top attraction. Besides, he likes to fight; maybe he thought the cats would give him a good workout."

"Did they?"

She laughed. "Monk says he scared them off just by yelling at them. Of course, you can't always believe what Monk says . . . and if Thaddeus' lips are moving, it's a fifty-fifty chance that he's lying." Her face clouded over with bitterness. "Especially if he's making promises."

She tossed the towel aside and started work on her stretching exercises. Houdini stared expressionlessly at her.

"Don't just stand there like a lump," she said. "I can talk and bend at the same time."

"I don't know quite what to say," he admitted.

"*That's* a novelty!" she laughed. "You've hardly shut up for the past four days."

"I can't help wondering why you maintain your daily

regimen with such vigor when it is apparent that you will not be performing."

"It's not apparent to *me*!" she snapped. "One of these days we're going to hit a world with humans, instead of just humanoids. I've got to keep fit."

He shook his head sadly. "When Mr. Ahasuerus says there are no such worlds, other than your own, he is telling the truth. Besides," he added with a smile, "I was raised to believe that *I* was a human and *you* were a humanoid."

"Really?"

He nodded his head. "It is the truth. Each race likes to think of itself as being in the true image of God, and views all other races as somehow aberrant. Mine is no different."

"You mean you believe in God?" she asked, surprised.

"Certainly," said Houdini. "Don't you?"

"I used to."

"It is curious," mused the magician. "The only member of your race who admits to the existence of God is Tojo, and yet he would seem to have less reason than any of the others."

"Because of the way he looks, you mean?" asked Gloria.

"And the way he sounds," agreed Houdini. "If he believes in God, then he must surely believe that God has deserted him. It would seem far more sensible for, say, Mr. Flint, an obviously successful man, to spend his days praising his God, and yet he scoffs at the concept."

"Thaddeus was never much for thanking *anyone*," replied Gloria wryly. "As for Tojo, he's probably the happiest person you know."

"Truly?"

"He spent his whole life looking for a family. Now he has one."

"I see," said the magician.

"Sometimes *I* don't," admitted Gloria. "Tojo can be totally satisfied just being among his friends."

"And you can't?"

"No offense, Houdini," she said. "But no, I can't. We're not all like that, you know. Look at Monk. He'd sooner risk his life against another Demoncat than stop being what he is.

Some people are only happy doing what they've been trained to do. It's all in how you look at it.''

"Despite the fact that your profession is considered degrading?'' asked Houdini.

"Who told you that?'' she demanded.

The magician looked flustered. "I've spoken to some of the others about it—just to try to understand your devotion to your craft.''

"Yeah? Well, Priscilla would degrade herself in two seconds flat if Thaddeus offered her a raise. She's done it before.''

"I meant no offense,'' said Houdini.

"I'm sure you didn't, but you have to understand that degradation is in the eye of the beholder. I never felt cheap or degraded when I was dancing, or even when I heard Thaddeus and some of the others discussing it. I can't help what they think. All I can do is be true to myself. I'm not like Tojo, or even you. Friends and security aren't enough for me. I want to do what I'm good at!''

"So do we all,'' he said gently.

"But most of you will settle for something else. I can't.''

"You feel I have settled for something less?'' he asked earnestly.

"Do you plan to stay with the show?''

"It is infinitely preferable to Kargennian's circus,'' he replied. "I am allowed to perform my illusions, the people are congenial, and I have made a friend. Yes, I plan to remain.''

"And you don't feel you've made any compromises?''

"No.''

"But you only perform for five minutes at a time, three shows a night,'' she pointed out.

"Mr. Flint feels that is all the audience will accept before becoming restless.''

"And you agree with him?'' she persisted.

"No. Not really,'' he admitted.

"But you don't fight it. You work less than two percent of each day, and you settle for it because it's better than being with Kargennian.''

"I never looked at it that way,'' he said, his face troubled.

"Do you try new tricks, new routines that push you to the limits of your abilities?"

"No, I do not."

"You *settle*," she repeated.

"But I am still a magician," he insisted defensively. "I still perform for an audience. I am not like Tojo in that respect."

She shook her head. "Tojo doesn't *want* to be a magician. He just wants to belong, and he'll put up with every kind of abuse Thaddeus can dish out for fear of losing what he's got."

"Yes, I see," he said thoughtfully. "I *am* much more like Tojo than like you."

"Cheer up," she said. "It's probably a lot more comfortable."

"Comfortable or not, it's *me*," he said with a wan smile. "What can I do?"

"If it's you, why do you want to do anything?" she replied.

"Because you make me feel guilty," he said. Then he shook his head. "No. You make me feel ashamed."

"Why? You're what you are. You can't be anything else. You're Houdini the Great, and at least you're working. *I'm* trying to be a Butterfly Delight, and I'm taking tickets from people who are paying to watch you and Monk and the Dancer."

"Then be Gloria."

"I tried," she said seriously. "I really did. And I found out what I guess I had known all along: Gloria's not worth being."

"She is my friend," Houdini said firmly.

"That's only because you're a funny-looking alien who walks on three legs and plays poker with the boys," she replied with a sad smile. "Once you've been around for a while, you won't like her or dislike her at all. You just won't think of her." She paused for a moment and gazed wistfully into the distance. "I wish you could have met Butterfly Delight."

"Maybe someday," he said quietly.

Gloria suddenly seemed oblivious to his presence, and after

132

a few minutes the magician sighed and wandered back to the Midway. Monk was medicating his leopards, Diggs was schooling his workers in some new scam or other, and Stogie was trying out a new pantomime routine on the Dancer, who watched him with a pleasant, impassive smile on his face.

Finally Houdini spied Flint and Mr. Ahasuerus walking toward the ship, and he approached them.

"Mr. Flint, I wish to have a word with you," he said harshly.

"I'll speak to you later," said the blue man to his partner, and started off toward the airlock.

"No," said Houdini. "This concerns you, too."

Mr. Ahasuerus stared at him, but said nothing.

"It's about Gloria," said the magician.

"I told you last night—" began Flint.

"I know what you told me last night," continued Houdini. "It is not good enough."

"I notice the word *sir* seems to have vanished from your vocabulary," remarked Flint, looking mildly amused.

"What is all this about, Mr. Flint?" inquired the blue man.

"Gloria's picked up a convert," replied Flint. "I suppose we're going to have to let her play to another empty house before he shuts up."

"No," said the magician. "But you can let her perform in the specialty show."

"And have everyone walk out before the Dancer arrives?" said Flint. "No chance, Houdini."

"Let her go on in *my* place," persisted Houdini.

"I already told you: *No*," said Flint. "Besides, you're a damned fine magician."

"It doesn't mean as much to me as her art does to her."

"You keep talking as if an audience wasn't involved," said Flint. "Look, if I could run her act at a loss, I'd do it, just to shut both of you up. But if she sees one more crowd get up and leave, she could wind up in a straitjacket."

"I am not familiar with that term."

"My partner is trying to say that one more rejection could well upset her mental balance," said the blue man gently. "Sadly, I must agree with him. Gloria is not a stable person."

"That's because she's not Gloria at all," said Houdini. "She is Butterfly Delight."

"You, too?" said Flint disgustedly. "Butterfly Delight is a goddamned stage name, nothing more."

"You are wrong!" snapped the magician. "It is the only real thing in her life!"

"The only goddamned reality that accrues to Butterfly Delight these days is that she's making the hired help awfully uppity!" snapped Flint.

Houdini turned to face the blue man. "I appeal to you, sir. Make him put her back in the show!"

"What can I say?" replied Mr. Ahasuerus with an eloquent shrug. "I agree with him."

"But you are different from him!" insisted Houdini. "You must be!"

The blue man shook his head. "We are two sides of a coin. He lacks empathy and tact, although he is slowly acquiring both. I lack drive and ambition, though I too am learning. We complement each other perfectly."

"Is there nothing I can say, no means by which I can supplicate you?" said the magician.

"Let Mr. Flint and myself discuss the matter in private," replied Mr. Ahasuerus. "Possibly there is a compromise to be discovered."

"Thank you, sir," said Houdini. He looked at Flint. "I apologize for my rudeness."

The magician turned and began walking back toward the knoll, his shoulders hunched, his head lowered.

"It's not just *her* anymore, Mr. Flint," said the blue man. "She is starting to affect the staff."

"I know," Flint responded with a grimace. "And if she can get an unaggressive guy like Houdini to start yelling at us, how long before Monk and his bear come around demanding Fair Play for Strippers?"

"Then shall we let her go back to performing?" mused Mr. Ahasuerus.

Flint shook his head. "I can't put her through that again. I wasn't kidding before—there's a chance she'll come unglued if audiences keep walking out on her. Things like that aren't supposed to happen to Butterfly Delight."

"Then what?" asked the blue man.

Flint lowered his head in thought for a moment, then suddenly looked up with a smile.

"You know, Mr. Ahasuerus, a change of scenery just might do her a world of good."

"What are you suggesting?" asked the blue man. "Returning her to Earth is out of the question."

"I know," replied Flint. "But she's not doing herself any good sitting around here moping day in and day out."

"Agreed."

"Look—the show can't spare you or me just now, not the way business has been picking up. And I'm sure as hell not about to let Monk spend five years hunting down a Red Devil. But sooner or later, *some*body's got to go out after Fast Johnny. Why not her?"

"You'd be sending one unstable personality out in search of another," replied Mr. Ahasuerus dubiously.

"I don't think so," said Flint. "She's only in danger of cracking up when she doesn't know who she is or whether she's worth anything. Give her a ship and a task and it just might convince her that she can be useful even if she keeps her clothes on."

"Can she pilot a ship?"

"What difference does it make?" replied Flint. "This isn't a game of hide-and-seek. We know where Fast Johnny is. Just program one of the robots to fly her there and back."

"Mr. Flint," said the blue man after considering the matter for a few moments, "I believe you may have hit upon a solution."

"Well," said Flint, "at least it can't hurt to give it a try."

"Indeed. It will give her time to collect her thoughts and distance herself from her problems, and even Houdini will have to acknowledge that we are making a sincere attempt to alleviate the situation. Mr. Flint, I think you have discovered an almost perfect compromise."

"I've been studying a master of the art," replied Flint with a smile. "When I haven't been trying to convert him, that is."

Shoulder to shoulder, the unlikely partners entered the ship and began making the necessary arrangements.

16.

The journey took five days at speeds that were many multiples of light. Gloria was resentful that the confines of the small ship were such that she was unable to exercise, and before long resentment had given way to claustrophobia. She wished that Mr. Ahasuerus had programmed the robot pilot to play cards or checkers, or at least to talk, though she couldn't imagine what she would have to talk about with a machine.

Finally, 117 hours into the voyage, the robot applied the braking mechanism, and as the universe once more became intelligible on the ship's viewing screen, she saw a large red star looming off in the distance, above her and to the right. They were approaching it so rapidly she was sure they would plunge right into it, but after another hour had passed she realized that they were going to slingshot around it. The robot chose an orbit almost two hundred million miles out from the star, and then she saw her destination: a brown planet, partially hidden from view by thick gray cloud cover. Again she had the feeling that the ship was moving too rapidly to avoid a disaster, and again she breathed a sigh of relief when it snapped around the planet as it had done with the star, and began orbiting it at a height of almost three hundred miles.

The orbit was rapid and eccentric, and she guessed that the ship's somewhat limited sensing devices were trying to find Carp's ship. It seemed an impossible task to her, but after seven orbits a number of lights began blinking on and off and the ship started descending.

She decided she would be happier if she didn't watch the ground come up to meet her, so she leaned back in her seat and closed her eyes until she felt the very gentle jarring sensation of touchdown and heard a number of the ship's systems begin clicking off.

Only then did she look at the viewscreen again, and what she saw filled her with dismay. How could Fast Johnny have chosen to stay on a world that looked like watery chocolate pudding—and how, given the size of that world, was she ever supposed to find him?

One of the ship's computer screens began flashing an atmospheric readout, but she paid no attention to it. The planet's oxygen-nitrogen content held no interest for her, and besides, Mr. Ahasuerus had already warned her that continued exposure to the air—anything over fifteen minutes—would prove hazardous. She had hoped to get away with just wearing a breathing mask, but then she noticed on another screen that the temperature was 16° centigrade. She didn't know what that translated into as Fahrenheit, but she decided to wear an entire spacesuit just to be on the safe side.

She pressed the button Flint had pointed out to her, and the ship produced a burst of high-pitched whistles, intended to be loud enough to draw the attention of any nearby natives. (He had explained, as gently as he could, that he didn't trust her to read a compass and didn't want her straying out of sight of the ship, and she had instantly agreed with no trace of embarrassment or humiliation.)

She pushed another button and the ship began sending out short-wave radio signals as well. Then, having nothing further to do, she watched the viewing screen and waited. She had a sinking feeling that it would take days before any inhabitants of the planet found the ship, but to her surprise she saw three enormous gray slugs slither into view within twenty minutes. She immediately donned her spacesuit, hooked up her translating devices—one for sending, one for receiving—and went out to meet them. (They had used only one device—a sender—at the carnival, but that was because Flint didn't much care what the marks said as long as they spent their money.)

"Hello," she said uneasily. "Can one of you tell me where I might find John Edward Carp?"

The three slugs responded with shrill hooting noises, and she realized that she had not activated the translating devices. She did so now, and repeated her question.

"One of us can," replied the nearest of the slugs.

Perhaps it was the way the translator worded the sentence, perhaps not. Certainly there was nothing human in the tone of the voice, nor any trace of humanity in the slug's body . . . but somehow she *knew*.

"Johnny?" she said hesitantly. "Is that you?"

"Hi, Gloria," replied the slug. "How's tricks?"

"My God—what have they done to you?"

Carp turned to his two companions. "You can leave us now," he said. "I'll be all right." He wriggled around and faced Gloria again, as the other two slugs crawled off into the slime and ooze of the planet's surface. "I figured Thaddeus would send someone after me before too much longer. That's why I've been hanging around the ship. *I* can tell the Hods apart, but I imagine we must all look alike to you."

"They're called Hods?"

"Yes. So am I, these days."

"I hardly know what to say," began Gloria. "They told me what you had become, but being told is one thing and seeing it with my own eyes is another."

"I wouldn't know about that," said Carp, wriggling closer. "I don't have eyes anymore."

"Oh!" said Gloria, startled. "I hadn't noticed."

"Don't let it upset you. There are compensations. I assume you're here for the ship?"

She nodded. "And for you."

"Good old Thaddeus!" said Carp, and from the way his body undulated she was sure he was laughing. "I'll bet he thinks he's going to hold me to my contract!"

"Johnny," said Gloria, "I know it's you, but would you stop coming so near to me? It makes me nervous."

"Anything you say," said Carp. "Well, give me your

sales pitch, get it over with, and then take the goddamned ship and go."

"You really don't want to come back?" she asked unbelievingly.

"To what? A five-and-dime carnival? I spent enough time looking at hicks and freaks. Now I've joined them."

"But why?"

Carp's entire body shivered as he emitted a long, hooting sigh. "You wouldn't understand."

"Try me."

"What the hell," said Carp. "You're probably the last human I've ever going to see, so why not? By the way, you don't happen to have a cigarette with you, do you?"

"I don't smoke," she replied. "It's bad for your cilia." Suddenly she was struck by the absurdity of lecturing a slug on the evils of tobacco.

"I don't even know if the new improved me *has* any cilia," said Carp. "Oh, well, it was a silly request at that. For all I know I might explode the second I took a puff. Damn, but I miss them! That's my only regret, Gloria—outside of the fact that I never got you into bed. Just tell me Thaddeus hasn't made it with you either, and all will be forgiven."

"He hasn't."

"Good." He paused. "Why are you smiling?"

"I thought you couldn't see," said Gloria.

"I don't have eyes. That's not quite the same thing."

"Oh," said Gloria, bewildered. "I was smiling because I'm sitting here on a strange world having a conversation with a gray slug who's dying for a cigarette and regrets not having gone to bed with me. I think that's pretty funny, don't you?"

"I suppose it is at that," admitted Carp. "You know, I never thought I was going to stay this way, not in the beginning. The only reason I volunteered was because the show was going broke playing the worlds Ahasuerus chose, and Thaddeus offered me too much to turn it down."

"Where did they do it to you?" she asked.

"A Corporate-owned hospital over on Zeta Piscium IX," replied Carp. "That was the closest one," he added. "I guess they've got about two hundred hospitals that can perform the operation."

"How long did it take?"

"Three weeks from start to finish. They tell me the usual surgery goes about half that time, but they really had their work cut out for them with me."

"Did it hurt much?" she asked, fascinated.

"Like hell itself," he said, and she was struck by the lack of emotion in his translated voice. "I cursed Thaddeus every second of every minute I was there. The doctors had told me there would be some pain involved. Hah! When a surgeon suggests that you might feel a bit of mild discomfort, you can bet your bottom dollar you're about to undergo the agony of the damned." He paused. "And after three weeks the pain was gone, and so was Fast Johnny Carp. They put me in my ship and set the navigational computer for Baxite."

"Baxite?"

"That's what the Hods call this place. I guess you were told it's Gamma Scuti IV. Anyway, I landed here and went out to convince the natives that they really wanted to play host to Thaddeus' carnival."

"But why *here*, of all places?"

"How the hell would I know? I'm just a two-bit advance man, Gloria. I do know they haven't been stockpiling any gold or diamonds or uranium. You'd have to ask Thaddeus or Ahasuerus or probably someone high up in the Corporation why this place means anything to them. All I know is why it's valuable to me."

"And why is that?"

"It feels good."

"I don't understand," said Gloria.

"I told you you wouldn't," said Carp. "I know it would sound better if I said they've got a utopian society going here, or that no one ever breaks the law, or that all the women are oversexed. But none of that's true. Actually, they're kind of primitive, and there are a hell of a lot of lawbreakers around, and I haven't had the slightest desire to roll in the hay—or the muck—with any of the women."

"Then *why*?"

"I know it's going to be hard for you to swallow, but I feel like a million dollars. I *like* being a Hod. I like the new senses they gave me, I like the way it feels when I wriggle around on the ground, I like the taste of the stuff I suck up through this thing that used to be my mouth. I know it must disgust you, but I feel happier and healthier than I've ever felt before."

"Have you a job?"

"Hell, no! Nobody has. What do I need money for? When I'm hungry I stop wherever I am and suck this stuff up. When I'm sleepy I burrow into the slime and let it cover me up. The Hods are friendly. They don't make any demands upon me, they accept me as one of them, and we get along fine."

"But who wants to sleep in slime?" she said, making a face.

"That's the translator screwing up," said Carp. "Let me see if I can rephrase it. To you, it's slime. To me, the way I am now, it's like a warm waterbed with satin sheets and goosefeather pillows. To you, I drink muck and filth; to me, it's like the finest dishes from Maxim's all laid out for me, waiting for my choice." He paused again. "How can I make it clear to you? Walking is nothing special. I did it every day of my life, and except for getting me from one place to another I never gave it any thought. But locomoting in this body is a sensual experience. It's like . . . I can't come up with an analogous word."

"Like an orgasm?" she suggested.

"No. That would drive anyone crazy. But it's like twenty-four hours a day of mild foreplay, if you see the difference."

"I suppose so," she replied dubiously. "And you're really hooked on this body?"

"Well, that's one way of putting it," said Carp. "I have no desire to ever leave it, that's for sure. I mean, what the hell is there to go back to, anyway? Just a bunch of misfits—begging your pardon, Gloria."

"But you were good at running the games," she said. "Almost as good as the Rigger."

"So what? They were just games." He paused. "Not everyone is as much in love with their professions as you are, Gloria. Some of us would rather just be happy."

"You make it seem very simple."

141

"It is. Why not spend a few months as a Hod and give it a try? I guarantee you'll like it. Who knows? I might finally get you under the covers—or the Hod equivalent of them."

"But I don't want to be a Hod," she said firmly.

"Then be whatever makes you happy."

"My work makes me happy."

"Well, I guess that's that," said Carp. "You can't be a stripper and a Hod at the same time. We don't wear any clothes." He paused. "I suppose I should be embarrassed about my nudity, but I know how Hods looked to me before I was one of them."

"They look different now?" asked Gloria slowly.

"Oh, yes. Nothing like becoming a member of a species to lose your distaste for their less elegant aspects. To be perfectly honest, I'm propositioning you mostly from memory; I've only been a Hod for a couple of months and already you appear . . . well, *alien*, if you know what I mean."

"You get assimilated that quickly?"

"*I* did," replied Carp. "But then, I *like* what I am. I seem to remember that Mr. Romany couldn't wait to stop looking like a Man."

"But it doesn't bother you at all?" she persisted.

"Not a bit. Look at how fast I learned the language. Oh, I took an intensive sleep-course in it on the way here, but that's not the same as actually making all these hooting sounds. I practically scared myself to death the first time I heard myself. Now I think it sounds kind of pretty."

"And there's no residual pain from the surgery?"

"Not a bit. I feel like . . . well, if I was still a Man, like I could screw all night long, play three quick sets of tennis in the morning, and then go out and run a marathon. Those surgeons know what they're doing, all right. They even fixed my asthma while they were at it."

"What did it cost?"

"I don't know. Thaddeus paid for it."

"Tell me more about the pain."

"What's there to tell? It hurt." He moved closer to her. "Don't tell me you're thinking of becoming a Hod!"

"No," she said slowly. "Not a Hod."

"But something?"

"I'm considering it."

"Well, hot damn! Now Thaddeus can't have you either!"

"He never could, Johnny," said Gloria. "Can they turn you into anything you want?"

"No. They can't make you a chlorine or methane breather, and I seem to remember them turning down some guy who wanted to move to a high-gravity world. They said they could make him look the part, but that his bones and muscles wouldn't be able to support him. But I could be wrong; I wasn't paying much attention." He raised his eyeless head and studied her. "Just out of curiosity, what do you want to become?"

"The same as you, Johnny," she answered him. "I want to become something I *like*."

"I always liked you just fine."

"You never knew me. You liked Butterfly Delight."

"Same difference," he replied.

"There's more difference than you can imagine. How far is it to Zeta Piscium?"

"I have no idea," he said. "My ship made it in about three days—but I still don't know why ships sometimes go at light speed and sometimes at fifty times light speed. In fact, there's a hell of a lot I don't know about this damned galaxy. Maybe that's why I like being a Hod: I get to sink into the ooze and not worry about stuff like that."

"Three days?" she repeated.

"*I* thought so—but hell, maybe it was nine. They changed my metabolism around to fit the world. It seems to me like a day and night are twelve hours apiece, but for all I know they're ten minutes or three weeks. That's what you've got to understand about the surgery. I'm not *like* a Hod; I *am* a Hod." He paused. "You might think about that before you make up your mind. If you go through with it, you won't just be Gloria Stunkel in a masquerade costume."

"That's fine by me," she said. "I never liked being Gloria Stunkel anyway."

"I think that's what I like best about you," said Carp.

"What?"

"You're even crazier than me."

"If I decide to go to Zeta Piscium, how do I get there from here?"

"Well, you can flap your arms real hard or you can take a spaceship—it's up to you."

"I see that becoming a Hod hasn't improved your sense of humor," she said dryly. "I don't know how to pilot a ship."

"How did you get here?"

"Mr. Ahasuerus programmed one of the robots to fly me here. Do you know how to reprogram it?"

"No—and even if I did, I'm no longer able to do any real delicate tinkering," answered Carp. He paused. "Wait a minute! I've got an idea. *Your* ship may not have the route to Zeta Piscium in its memory banks, but *mine* sure as hell does. You can have the robot fly your ship back to wherever the show is at and take mine."

"I still don't know how to fly it."

"I can't *show* you," said Carp, "but I can *tell* you. It's not that difficult. The navigational computer does just about everything except land it."

"I can't land a ship!" protested Gloria. "I don't even know how to drive a car!"

"It's up to you," said Carp. "Just how badly do you want to stop being Gloria and become whatever it is that seems to appeal to you so much?"

"Bad enough," she responded at last. "How long will it take for you to teach me?"

"An hour, a day, a week—who the hell knows? You've been Gloria Stunkel all your life; can you keep being her for as long as it takes to learn."

"All right. Where is your ship? It must be close by, or the robot wouldn't have landed here."

"About two miles away," said Carp. "But we don't have to go there yet. I can explain how it works while we're here, where you'll be comfortable. *My* ship was remodeled, so to speak, for my new image."

"Yes, but your ship has a radio I can use without spending hours convincing the robot that I've got a message worth sending."

"And who do you want to talk to?"

"Thaddeus."

"All right," said Carp. "Follow me. We'll be going through what passes for lush vegetation on this world, but don't worry. Even if you lose sight of me, I'm not the fastest-moving thing you've ever seen."

They set off for Carp's ship together, and within half a mile Gloria was sinking up to her knees in the mire with every step. Carp offered to let her ride on his back, but somehow the thought of making physical contact with him was more repulsive than foot-slogging through her surroundings, and she declined the offer.

It took them almost three hours to cover the distance, but at last they reached the ship, and Carp entered it first.

"I know you aren't thrilled by my proximity," he explained, "but the radio is also rigged for a Hod. I'll get it homed in and then you can take over."

He spent a few minutes adjusting various dials and buttons and then slithered back down to the ground.

"It's all yours," he said. "Press the blue button when you want to speak. This is going on subspace tightbeam, which mean it's pretty damned fast, but it's still going to take five or six minutes for you to get an answer to anything you say."

"Thank you, Johnny," she said, stepping around his pulsating bulk and climbing the stairs to the pilot's cabin. They took a bit of negotiating, since they were made for a Hod, but finally she reached the radio and pushed the blue button.

"Thaddeus. This is Gloria. Can you hear me?"

"It's going to take him a while to answer, even if he's sitting right next to the radio," remarked Carp. "Want to play Three Thirds of a Ghost while we're waiting?"

She shook her head and stared intently at the radio. Just when she was sure it wasn't working. Flint's voice came over the speaker, crackling with static.

"This is Thaddeus. Mr. Ahasuerus says that it takes forever to hold a conversation on these things, so let me ask you a batch of questions at once. Did you find Fast Johnny? Is he okay? Are you okay? When will you be coming back? And is he coming with you?" Then, as an afterthought: "Oh, yeah—Tojo says hello."

"Yes, I found fast Johnny, and no, he's not coming back with me," replied Gloria. "And, while we're on the subject, I'm not coming back either. But don't worry, Thaddeus—I'm not going native. In fact, I've got a little business proposition for you. . . ."

17.

"Look at it, Thaddeus!" exclaimed Tojo, standing at the base of their two-man ship. "It's fabulous!"

"Somehow I'm not surprised," replied Flint, climbing down the stairs and joining him. He paused to activate his sending and receiving translators.

"Oh? Had Houdini described it to you?"

"No," said Flint, looking at the sprawling megalopolis that crept up to the edge of the spaceport. "But Mr. Ahasuerus has never expressed any interest in playing the Hesporite system, so it stood to reason that they've got lots of people and a thriving economy." He lit an artificial cigarette and tried not to cough.

Three months had passed since he had agreed to Gloria's deal, during which time the carnival had crawled out of the red and into the black, and he had managed to get Kargennian to spring for two more rides and another dozen games workers. The Dancer was still playing to packed houses, Stogie was pulling in an extra two to three thousand customers per night, and Julius Squeezer's record now stood at 308 wins against only 17 defeats. Except for the death of Monk's leopards, things couldn't have gone much more smoothly, and Flint had finally decided to take a few days off to check out his most recent investment.

"I'm surprised someone's not here to meet us," remarked Tojo, looking around.

"If this were a science fiction story," said Flint, scanning the huge number of boulevards that converged about a half mile from them, "I'd say the aliens were giving us a survival test. Oh, well," he added with a shrug, "we might as well announce ourselves."

He pulled a pistol out of his pocket and fired it into the air.

"*That* ought to get a response," he said with a smile.

"I didn't know you owned a gun, Thaddeus," said the hunchback.

"I borrowed it from the Dancer."

"But why?"

"You never know when you're going to need one."

"But Hesporite III is a member of the Community of Worlds! Surely you don't expect any trouble here!"

"Tojo, there are carny people, and there's everyone else. You can't trust half the carnies you know, and you can't trust none of the rest of 'em." He fired the pistol again. "If someone doesn't come by pretty damned soon, I'm going to aim the next shot at something breakable."

Suddenly a small open vehicle approached them, driven by a member of Houdini's race.

"I must inform you that weaponry of any type is illegal on Hesporite III," said the driver as the vehicle came to a stop.

"This?" asked Flint into his translator, holding his pistol up. "It's just a noisemaker."

"I am afraid I must examine it, sir," replied the driver.

"Tell you what," said Flint. "You point out the way to *The Seven-Star Carnival*, and you can keep the goddamned thing."

"I must confiscate it regardless," said the driver, "but once you give it to me, I will be happy to ferry you to a public conveyance and give you directions to your location."

Flint shrugged, handed over the pistol, and clambered into the vehicle after first boosting Tojo onto the back seat.

They were driven to a train, which obviously terminated at the spaceport, and told to get off at the tenth stop. The seats were not made for humans, and they elected to stand for the duration of the journey. Aliens were not unknown on Hesporite III, but they were still rare enough so the two humans got more than their share of curious stares during the trip.

148

Finally they got off and followed the signs—the writing was unintelligible, but the illustrations were quite adequate— and within a mile they had come to the carnival, which had set up shop in the Hesporitan equivalent of a cornfield.

"Lousy games," said Flint, surveying the Midway with a practiced eye. "I guess these guys never heard what old P.T. had to say about suckers and even breaks."

"It seems clean, though," remarked Tojo. "And they have some nice rides."

"No freak show," said Flint. "Jesus! You'd think they'd be easy to put together with a whole galaxy to choose from."

"I think I've found what we're looking for!" exclaimed Tojo suddenly. He pointed to a tent about two hundred feet distant, with a huge illustration of a magician pulling some kind of alien animal out of a hat.

"Looks like it," agreed Flint.

They walked up to the tent, paid their admissions after waiting a few minutes to find out the current value of a credit on Hesporite, and entered.

Houdini was standing on a makeshift stage, producing bouquets out of empty air with wild abandon, and even incorporating some tricks with one of the Rigger's old decks of cards.

"Full house," whispered Tojo, after doing a quick head count. "About three hundred."

Flint nodded, and concentrated on the magician. Houdini took about ten minutes to work his way through his repertoire of illusions, then stepped forward to a microphone.

"And now, the moment you've all been waiting for," he announced, as the crowd suddenly became more attentive. "Presenting the first ecdysiast in the history of Hesporite: the one, the only, the fabulous Butterfly Delight!"

The lights dimmed, the music began, and a single spotlight hit the stage as Butterfly Delight stepped out and strutted to the center amid a wild cheer from the crowd.

"That's not her," whispered Tojo. "It can't be!"

"Shut up and watch," answered Flint.

The dancer's features were still humanoid, but there was no trace of Gloria Stunkel in them. Her eyes, like Houdini's, were small and wide-set; her ears were large and set low on her head; her arms seemed to be jointed at slightly different places; and of course she had the same tripodal structure as the other members of the race.

The three-legged hootch dancer started bumping and shimmying to the music—alien music, but with a primal beat that seemed universal—and the audience went crazy, filling the air with hoots and whistles and cheers. She removed a glove and threw it to them, and a fight almost broke out for possession of it.

"They like her, Thaddeus!" whispered Tojo excitedly. "They really like her!"

Flint grunted an affirmative and kept his eyes on the dancer. Some of her moves had changed because of the nature of her new body, but as the act continued he started noticing little touches that had carried over: the double bumps in time with the snare drum, the false modesty until the audience literally begged her to remove her last few pieces of clothing, the way she clung to the curtains. The floor work was gone—her three-legged body couldn't adapt to it—but she had some interesting moves in its place.

Finally the performance was over, and the dancer struck a pose, waited for the ovation to die down, bowed once, and stepped back behind the curtain.

Flint waited until the tent had emptied out, then climbed onto the stage, helped Tojo up onto it, and felt behind the curtains until he came to a flap in the canvas structure.

He stepped through, and found the dancer seated on an incredibly complicated chair, a satin robe wrapped around her sweating body, looking into a mirror as she removed her makeup.

"Not bad for a broad with three legs," said Flint softly.

She turned suddenly to face him.

"Thaddeus!" she cried happily in English. "Did you see the show?"

Flint nodded. "Tojo doesn't believe it's you."

"It's me, all right," she replied with an alien smile. "Hello, Tojo. How are you?"

"Fine, Gloria," stammered the hunchback. "And you?"

"Better than I've ever been," she said. She turned back to

150

Flint. "Did you see the audience, Thaddeus? Did you hear them?"

"Yes."

"They've been like this since we got here! Two religious groups have even tried to shut us down. It's just like the old days!"

"*It* is," said Flint. "*You* aren't."

"You're not backing down on our deal?" she said quickly.

He smiled. "No. I like what I saw."

"Then we can stay in business?"

Flint nodded. "We'll pick up the tab for the surgery and bankroll the show in exchange for half the profits."

"I *knew* you'd go for it if you saw the show!" she exclaimed, smiling happily.

"Just one thing troubles me," said Flint.

"What?"

"Well, everything is new and exciting to you now, but you weren't born in this body, and sooner or later I think you're going to get tired of it. What happens then?"

"She can always become one of us again," put in Tojo.

She shook her head. "Never again. But if I get tired of being a three-legged stripper, I've got the whole galaxy to choose from. There's thousands of races out there, Thaddeus. Maybe I'll become a lizard and shed my skin. Maybe I'll be a bird and molt to music. Who knows? But it's all there for the taking. As long as I can work and make audiences happy, I'm never changing back."

"Well, that's it," said Flint. He leaned over and kissed her on a leathery cheek. "Good luck, Gloria."

"Gloria was a dull little stumblebum that nobody wanted," she corrected him, still smiling. "I'm Butterfly Delight."

"I guess you finally are," admitted Flint.

18.

"Well, at least she is happy," said Mr. Ahasuerus, sitting behind his desk and sipping from his ever-present cup of coffee. Flint was sprawled on his partner's couch, while Tojo, unable to make himself comfortable on any of the furnishings, stood by the doorway.

"She's more than happy," replied Flint. "She's a goddamned star. She's going to make us almost as much money as the Dancer."

"Who would have thought it?" mused Mr. Ahasuerus. "Our Gloria!"

"She may be *ours*," said Flint, "but she's not Gloria. Not any longer."

They fell silent for a moment while Flint lit a cigarette, coughed once, and made a face.

"Are you *ever* going to teach those idiot robots how to make one of these things?"

"They do their best," said the blue man.

"I notice they didn't have any trouble synthesizing decent coffee for *you*," muttered Flint.

"Well," sighed Mr. Ahasuerus, "at least we're back to problems that we're used to. I'll reprogram the galley robots tomorrow morning."

"See that you do," said Flint. Suddenly he grinned. "It *does* beat the hell out of identity crises, doesn't it?"

"Indeed it does," replied the blue man, exposing his teeth in his equivalent of a smile. "I assume everybody here knows who he is?"

"Sure," said Tojo. "I'm the person Thaddeus yells at."

"And I'm the guy who yells at the dwarf," responded Flint easily. He turned to Mr. Ahasuerus. "What about you?"

"I'm the one who puts up with all of this and wonders why," replied the blue man with a weariness that didn't quite mask his delight.

ABOUT THE AUTHOR

MIKE RESNICK was born in Chicago in 1942, attended the University of Chicago (where, in the process of researching his first adventure novel, he earned three letters on the fencing team and was nationally ranked for a brief period), and married his wife, Carol, in 1961. They have one daughter, Laura.

From the time he was 22, Mike has made his living as a professional writer. He and Carol have also been very active at science fiction conventions, where Mike is a frequent speaker and Carol's stunning costumes have swept numerous awards at masquerade competitions.

Mike and Carol were among the leading breeders and exhibitors of show collies during the 1970s, a hobby which led them to move to Cincinnati and purchase a boarding and grooming kennel.

Mike has received several awards for his short stories and an award for a nonfiction book for teenagers. His first love, though, remains science fiction, and his excellent science fiction novels— THE SOUL EATER, BIRTHRIGHT: THE BOOK OF MAN, WALPURGIS III, and SIDESHOW— are also available in Signet editions.